BATMAN TEENAGE MUTANT NINJA TURTLES ADVENTURES

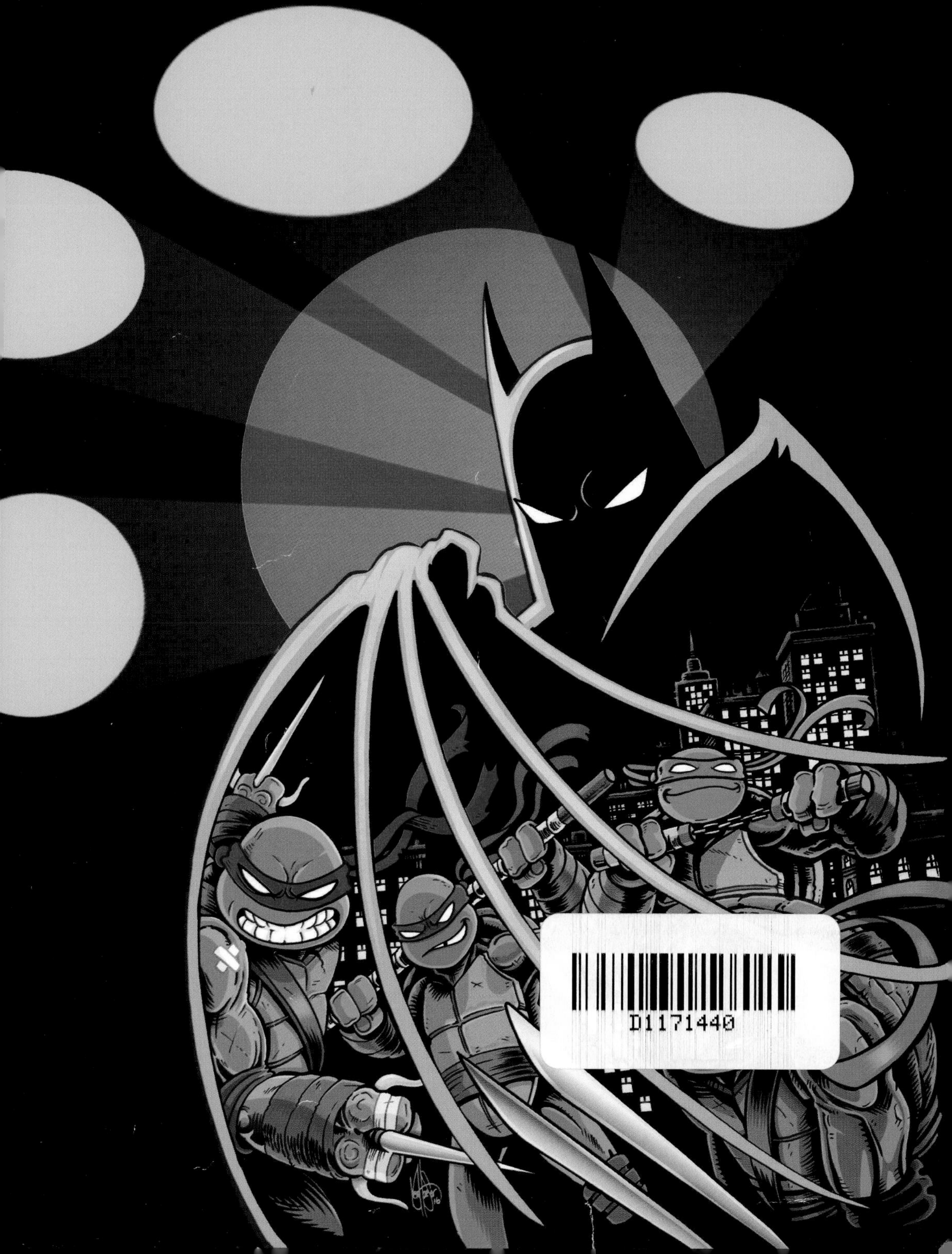

Batman / Teenage Mutant Ninja Turtles Advetnures
is published by Stone Arch Books,
A Capstone Imprint
1710 Roe Crest Drive
North Mankato, Minnesota 56003
www.mycapstonepub.com

Originally published as BATMAN/TEENAGE MUTANT NINJA
TURTLES ADVENTURES issue #2.

Special thanks to Jim Chadwick, Joan Hilty, Linda Lee,
and Kat van Dam for their invaluable assistance. All
rights reserved. No part of this publication may be
produced in whole or in part, or stored in a retrieval
system, or transmitted in any form or by any means,
electronic, mechanical, photocopying, recording, or
otherwise, without written permissions of the publisher.

Cataloging-in-Publication Data is available at the
Library of Congress website:
ISBN 978-1-4965-7382-7 (library binding)
ISBN 978-1-4965-7390-2 (eBook PDF)

Summary: Harley Quinn and The Joker escape Arkham
Prison and arrive in New York City. There, they team up
with super-villain Shredder. Batman and the Teenage
Mutant Ninja Turtles will have to join forces to stop the
deadly trio.

STONE ARCH BOOKS
Donald Lemke Editorial Director
Gena Chester Editor
Hilary Wacholz Art Director
Kathy McColley Production Specialist

Batman created by Bob Kane with Bill Finger

BATMAN TEENAGE MUTANT NINJA TURTLES ADVENTURES

THE CLOWN AND THE CLAN

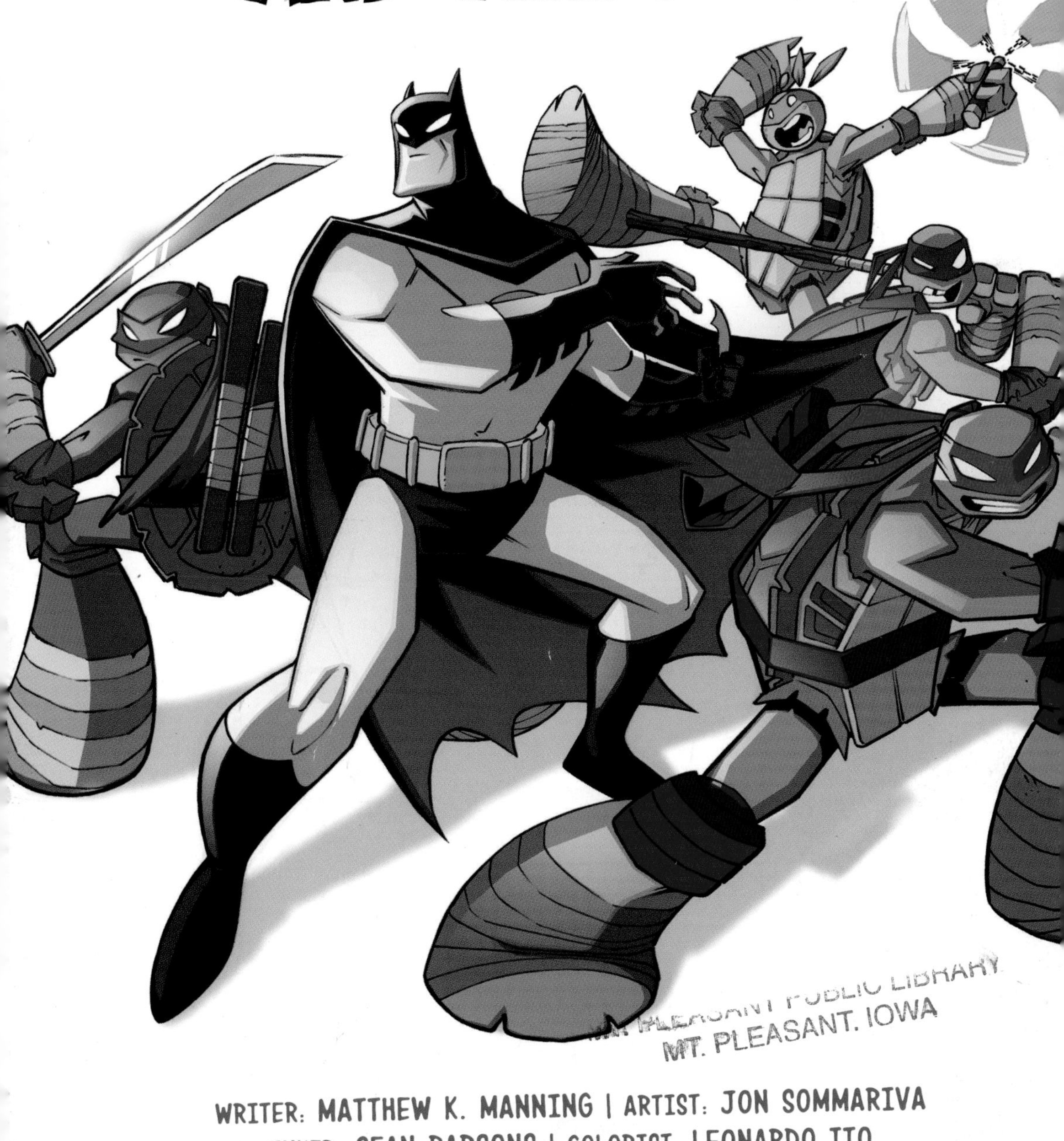

WRITER: MATTHEW K. MANNING | ARTIST: JON SOMMARIVA
INKER: SEAN PARSONS | COLORIST: LEONARDO ITO

STONE ARCH BOOKS
a capstone imprint

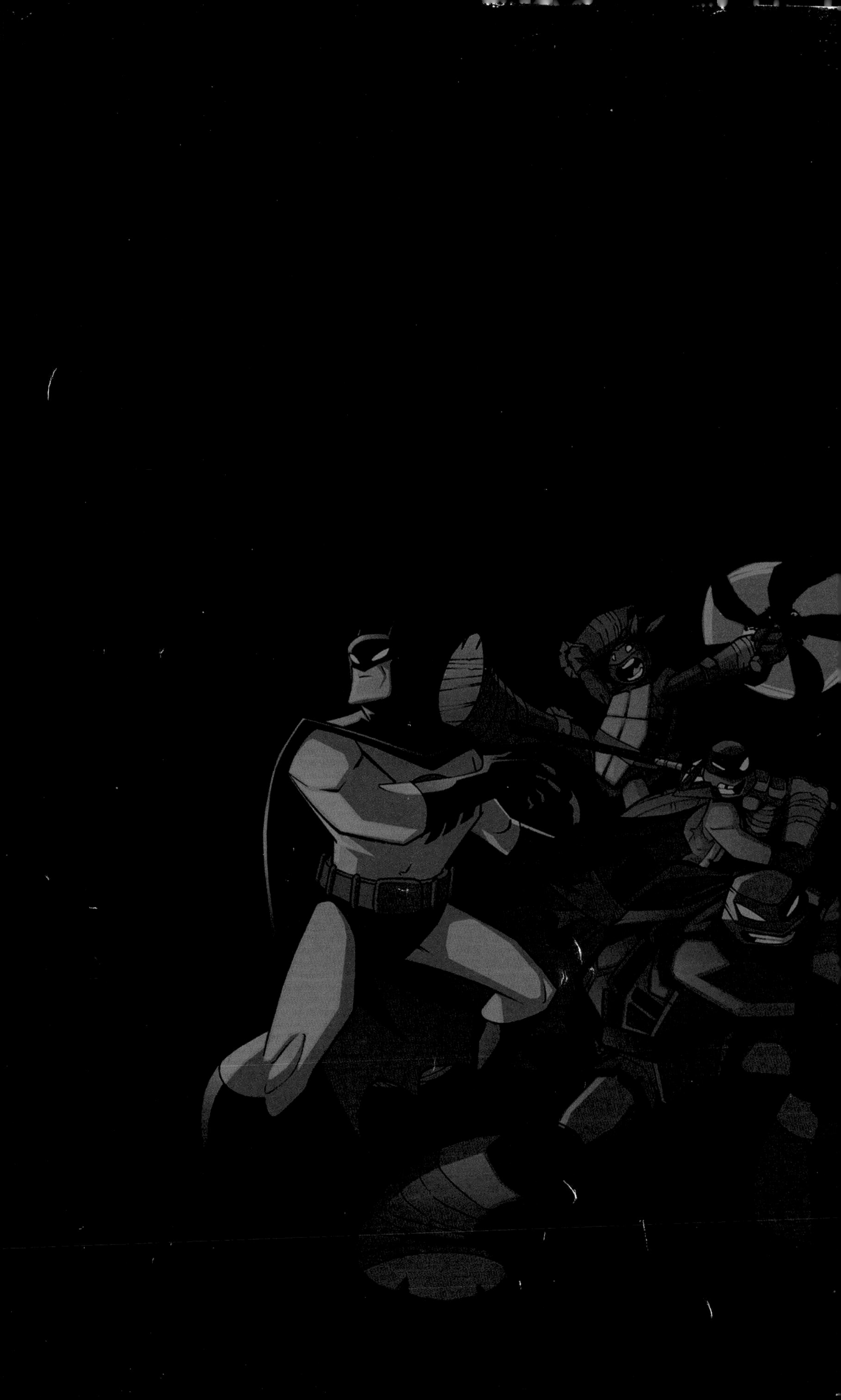

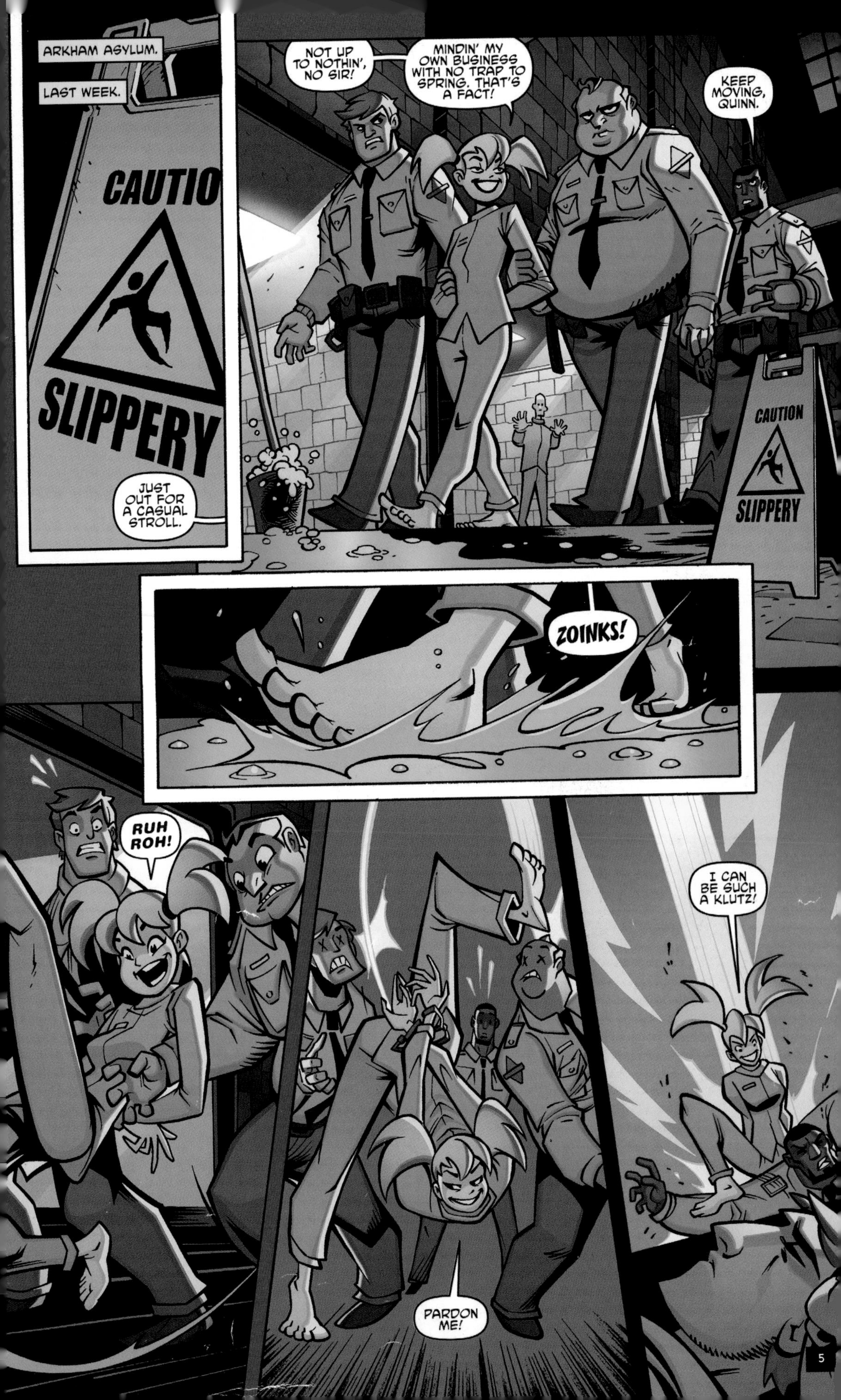
ARKHAM ASYLUM.
LAST WEEK.
CAUTION
SLIPPERY
NOT UP TO NOTHIN', NO SIR!
MINDIN' MY OWN BUSINESS WITH NO TRAP TO SPRING. THAT'S A FACT!
KEEP MOVING, QUINN.
JUST OUT FOR A CASUAL STROLL.
CAUTION
SLIPPERY
ZOINKS!
RUH ROH!
PARDON ME!
I CAN BE SUCH A KLUTZ!

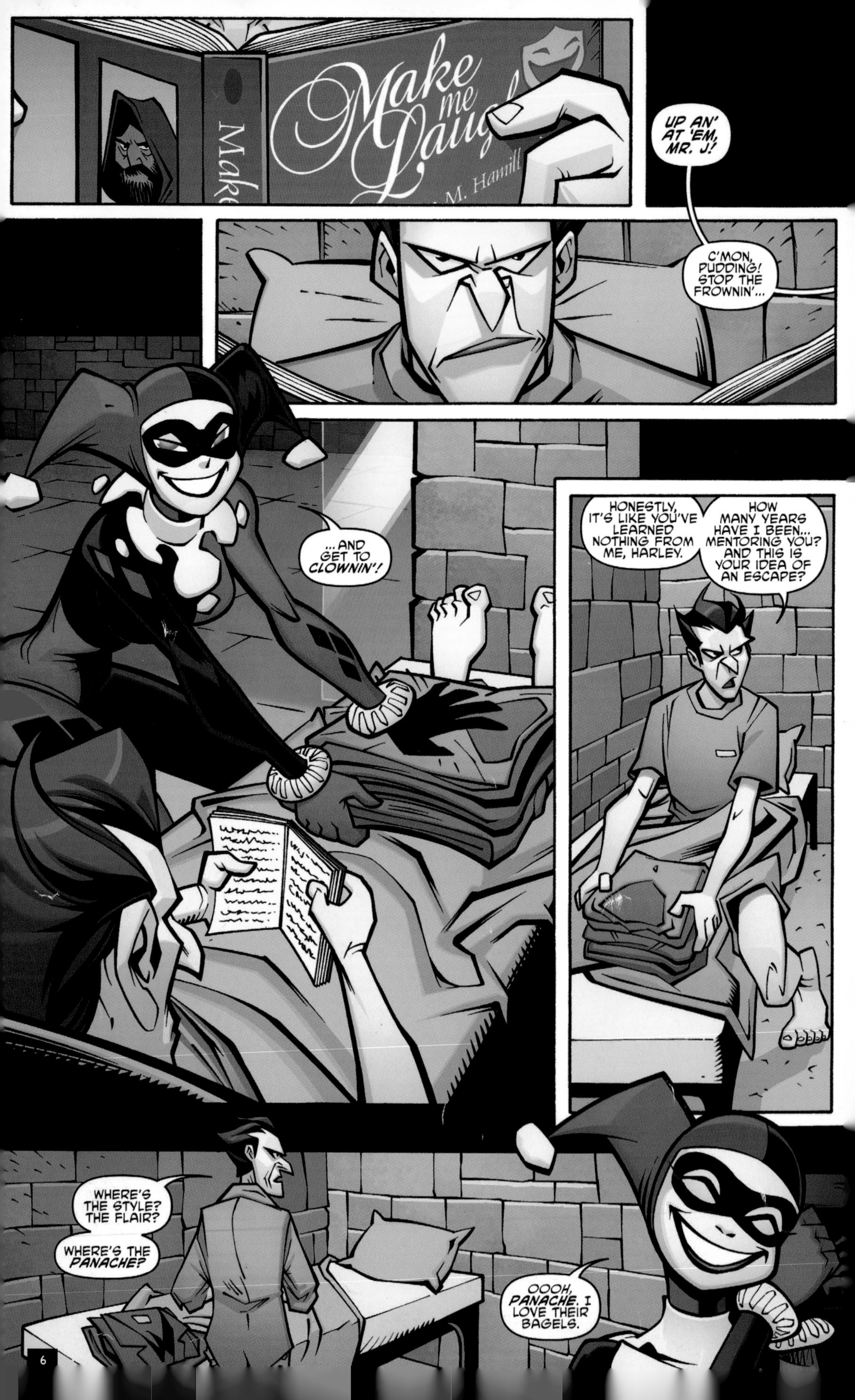

Make me Laugh
M. Hamill
Make
UP AN' AT 'EM, MR. J!
C'MON, PUDDING! STOP THE FROWNIN'...
...AND GET TO CLOWNIN'!
HONESTLY, IT'S LIKE YOU'VE LEARNED NOTHING FROM ME, HARLEY.
HOW MANY YEARS HAVE I BEEN... MENTORING YOU? AND THIS IS YOUR IDEA OF AN ESCAPE?
WHERE'S THE STYLE? THE FLAIR?
WHERE'S THE PANACHE?
OOOH, PANACHE. I LOVE THEIR BAGELS.

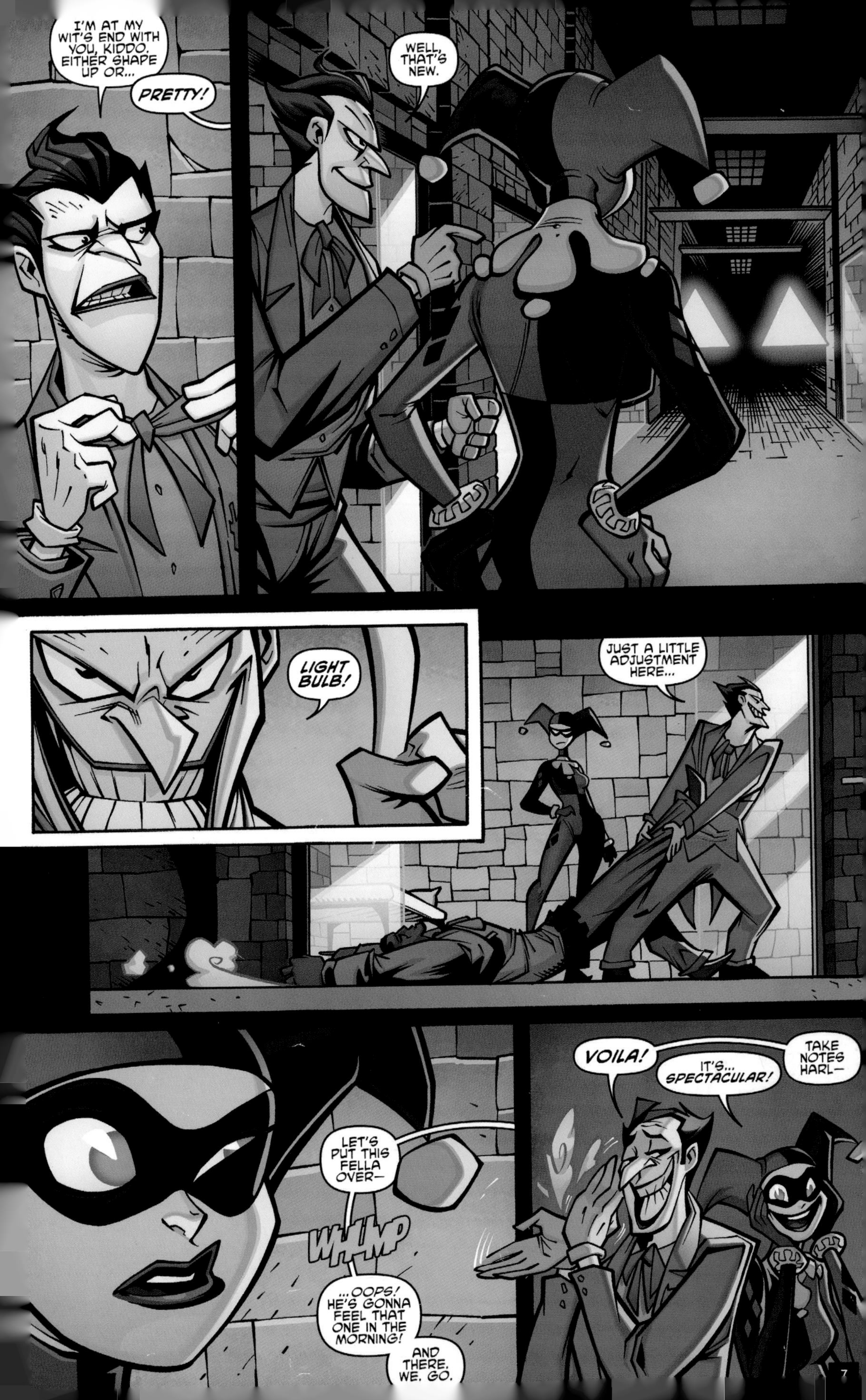
I'M AT MY WIT'S END WITH YOU, KIDDO. EITHER SHAPE UP OR...
PRETTY!
WELL, THAT'S NEW.
LIGHT BULB!
JUST A LITTLE ADJUSTMENT HERE...
LET'S PUT THIS FELLA OVER—
WHUMP
...OOPS! HE'S GONNA FEEL THAT ONE IN THE MORNING!
AND THERE. WE. GO.
VOILA!
IT'S... SPECTACULAR!
TAKE NOTES HARL—

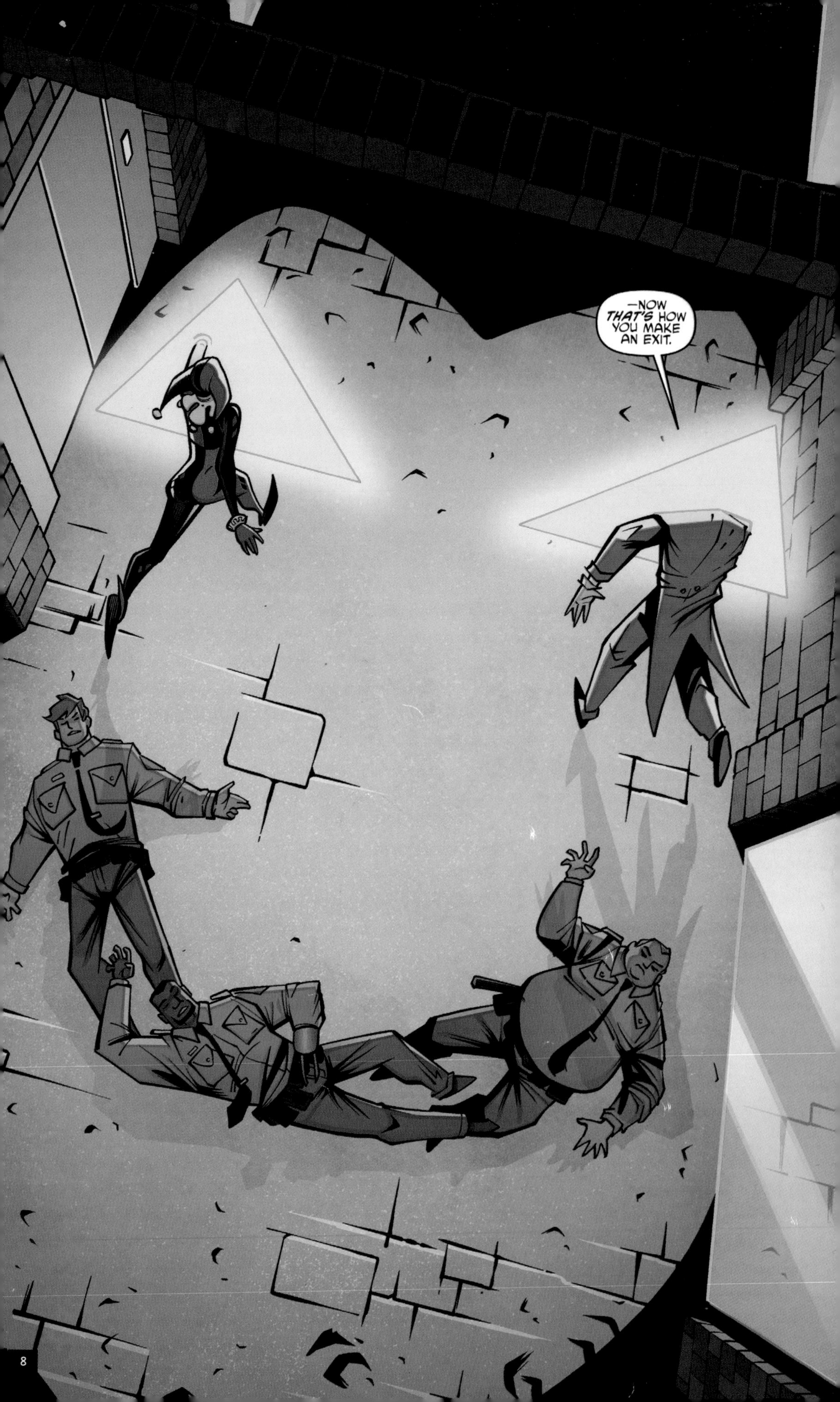
—NOW *THAT'S* HOW YOU MAKE AN EXIT.

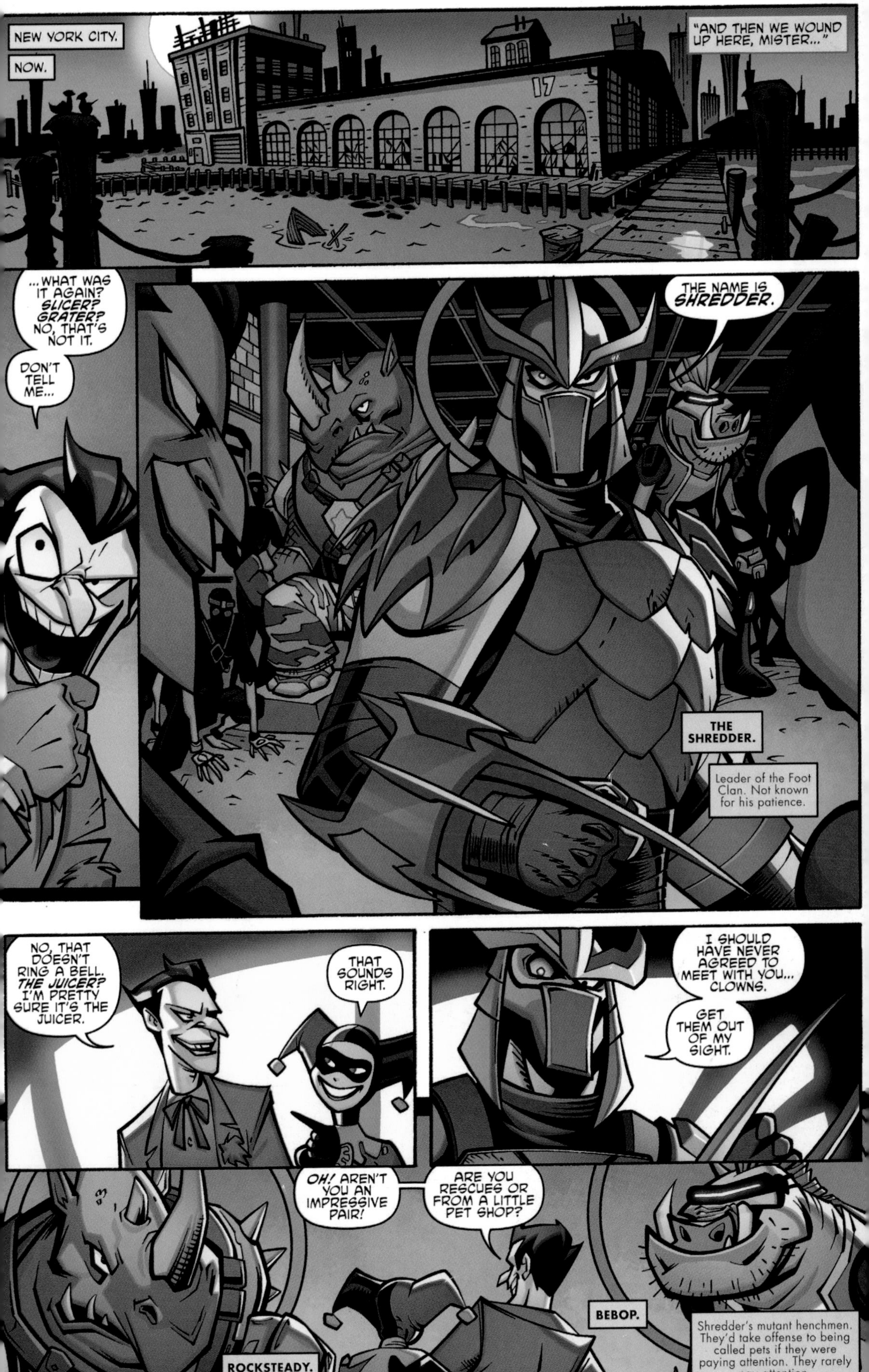

NEW YORK CITY.
NOW.
"AND THEN WE WOUND UP HERE, MISTER..."
...WHAT WAS IT AGAIN? SLICER? GRATER? NO, THAT'S NOT IT.
DON'T TELL ME...
THE NAME IS SHREDDER.
THE SHREDDER.
Leader of the Foot Clan. Not known for his patience.
NO, THAT DOESN'T RING A BELL. THE JUICER? I'M PRETTY SURE IT'S THE JUICER.
THAT SOUNDS RIGHT.
I SHOULD HAVE NEVER AGREED TO MEET WITH YOU... CLOWNS.
GET THEM OUT OF MY SIGHT.
OH! AREN'T YOU AN IMPRESSIVE PAIR!
ARE YOU RESCUES OR FROM A LITTLE PET SHOP?
BEBOP.
ROCKSTEADY.
Shredder's mutant henchmen. They'd take offense to being called pets if they were paying attention. They rarely pay attention.

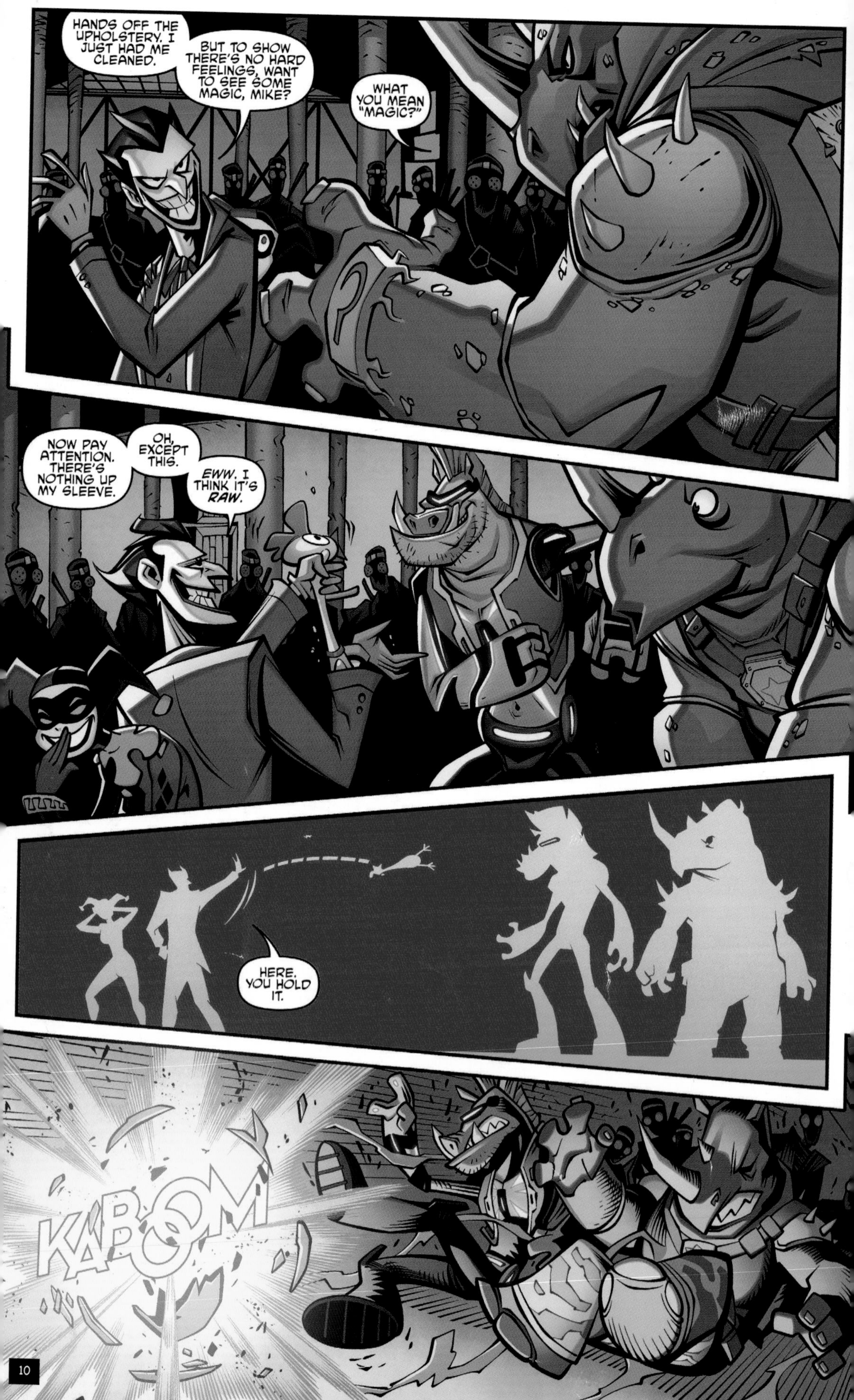

HANDS OFF THE UPHOLSTERY. I JUST HAD ME CLEANED.
BUT TO SHOW THERE'S NO HARD FEELINGS, WANT TO SEE SOME MAGIC, MIKE?
WHAT YOU MEAN "MAGIC?"
NOW PAY ATTENTION. THERE'S NOTHING UP MY SLEEVE.
OH, EXCEPT THIS.
EWW. I THINK IT'S *RAW*.
HERE. YOU HOLD IT.
KABOOM

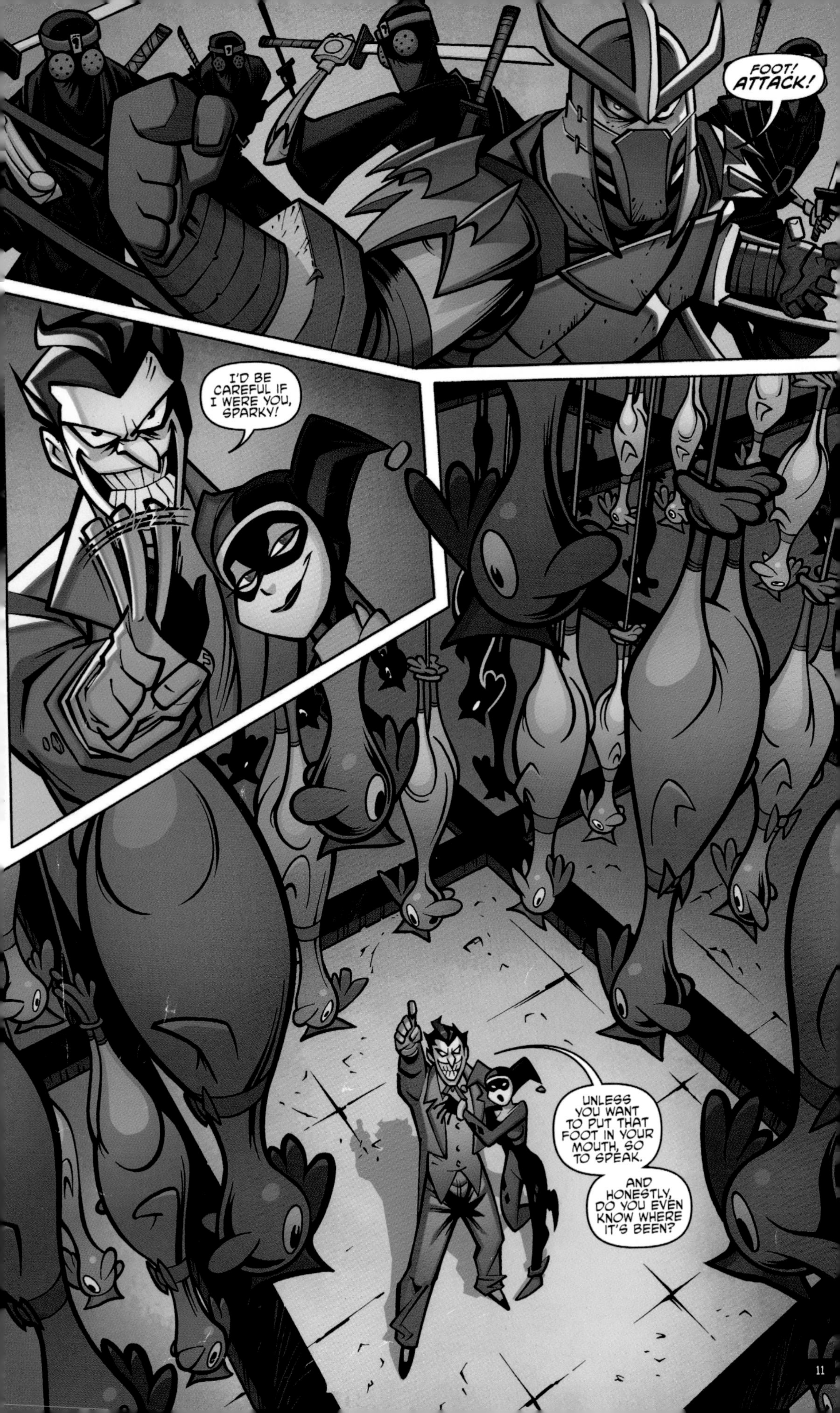
FOOT! ATTACK!
I'D BE CAREFUL IF I WERE YOU, SPARKY!
UNLESS YOU WANT TO PUT THAT FOOT IN YOUR MOUTH, SO TO SPEAK.
AND HONESTLY, DO YOU EVEN KNOW WHERE IT'S BEEN?

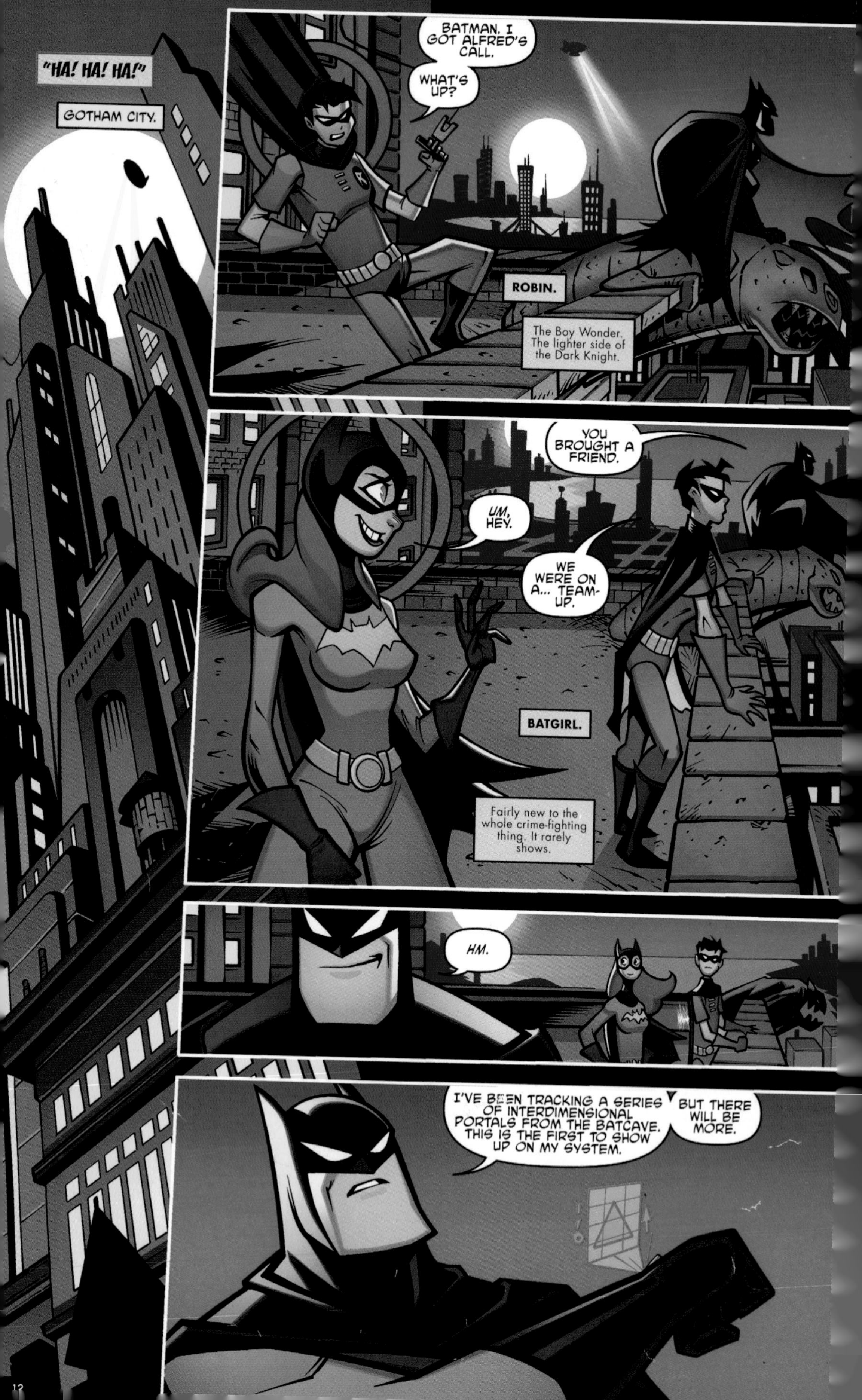
"HA! HA! HA!"
GOTHAM CITY.
BATMAN. I GOT ALFRED'S CALL.
WHAT'S UP?
ROBIN.
The Boy Wonder. The lighter side of the Dark Knight.
YOU BROUGHT A FRIEND.
UM, HEY.
WE WERE ON A... TEAM-UP.
BATGIRL.
Fairly new to the whole crime-fighting thing. It rarely shows.
HM.
I'VE BEEN TRACKING A SERIES OF INTERDIMENSIONAL PORTALS FROM THE BATCAVE. THIS IS THE FIRST TO SHOW UP ON MY SYSTEM.
BUT THERE WILL BE MORE.

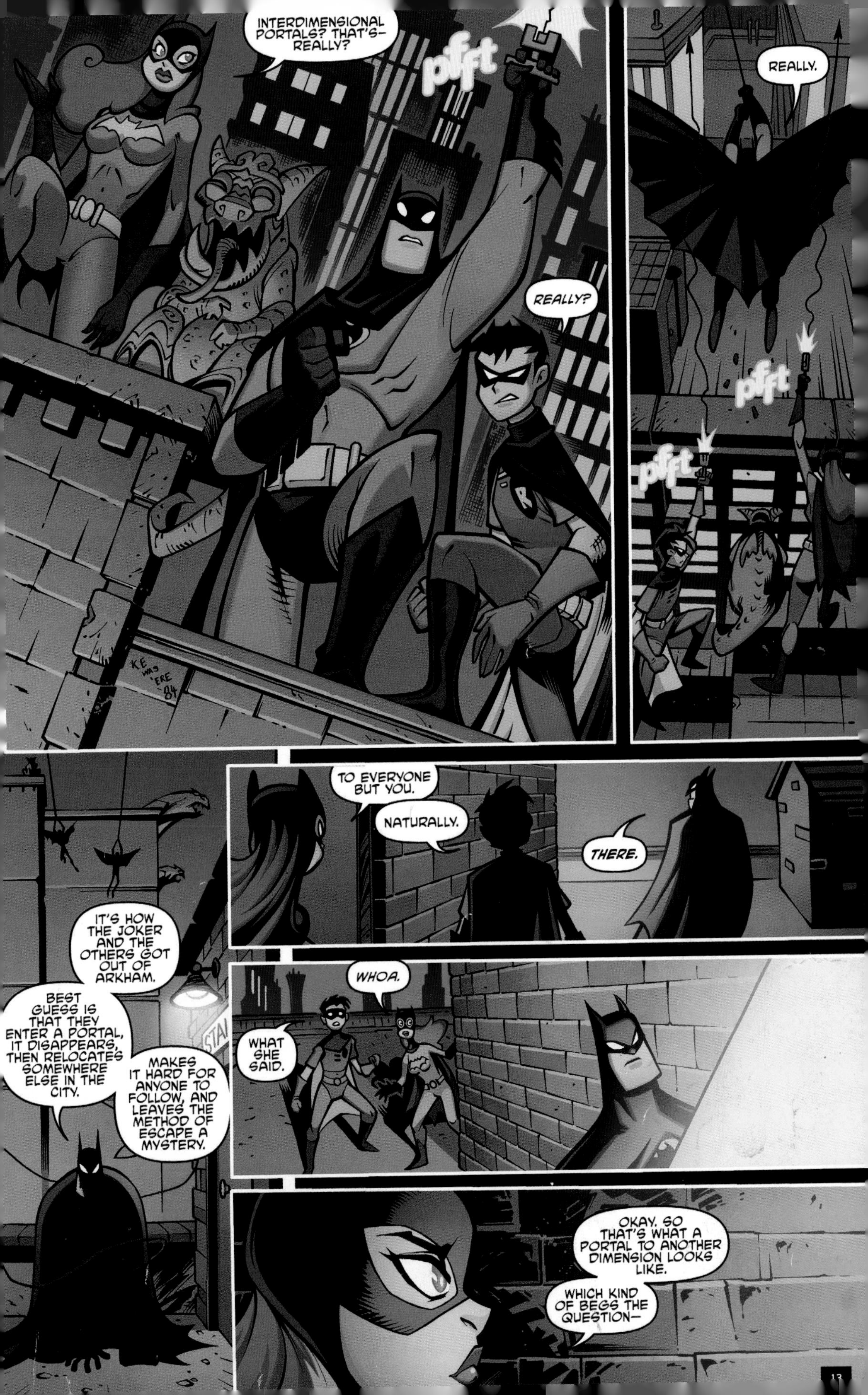

INTERDIMENSIONAL PORTALS? THAT'S— REALLY?
pfft
REALLY?
REALLY.
pfft
pfft
KE was 'ERE '84
IT'S HOW THE JOKER AND THE OTHERS GOT OUT OF ARKHAM.
BEST GUESS IS THAT THEY ENTER A PORTAL, IT DISAPPEARS, THEN RELOCATES SOMEWHERE ELSE IN THE CITY.
MAKES IT HARD FOR ANYONE TO FOLLOW, AND LEAVES THE METHOD OF ESCAPE A MYSTERY.
TO EVERYONE BUT YOU.
NATURALLY.
THERE.
WHOA.
WHAT SHE SAID.
OKAY. SO THAT'S WHAT A PORTAL TO ANOTHER DIMENSION LOOKS LIKE.
WHICH KIND OF BEGS THE QUESTION—

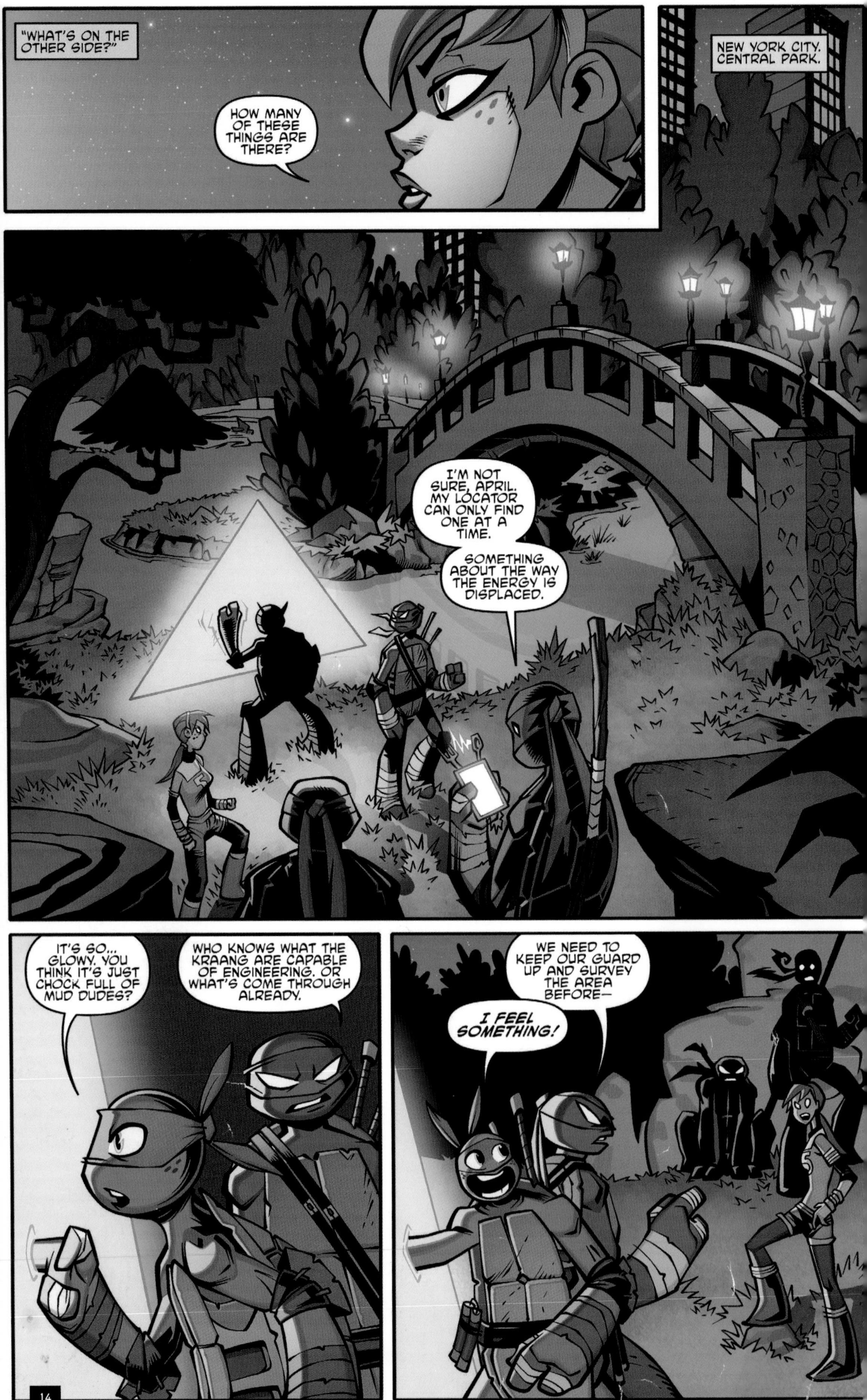

"WHAT'S ON THE OTHER SIDE?"
HOW MANY OF THESE THINGS ARE THERE?
NEW YORK CITY. CENTRAL PARK.
I'M NOT SURE, APRIL. MY LOCATOR CAN ONLY FIND ONE AT A TIME.
SOMETHING ABOUT THE WAY THE ENERGY IS DISPLACED.
IT'S SO... GLOWY. YOU THINK IT'S JUST CHOCK FULL OF MUD DUDES?
WHO KNOWS WHAT THE KRAANG ARE CAPABLE OF ENGINEERING. OR WHAT'S COME THROUGH ALREADY.
WE NEED TO KEEP OUR GUARD UP AND SURVEY THE AREA BEFORE—
I FEEL SOMETHING!

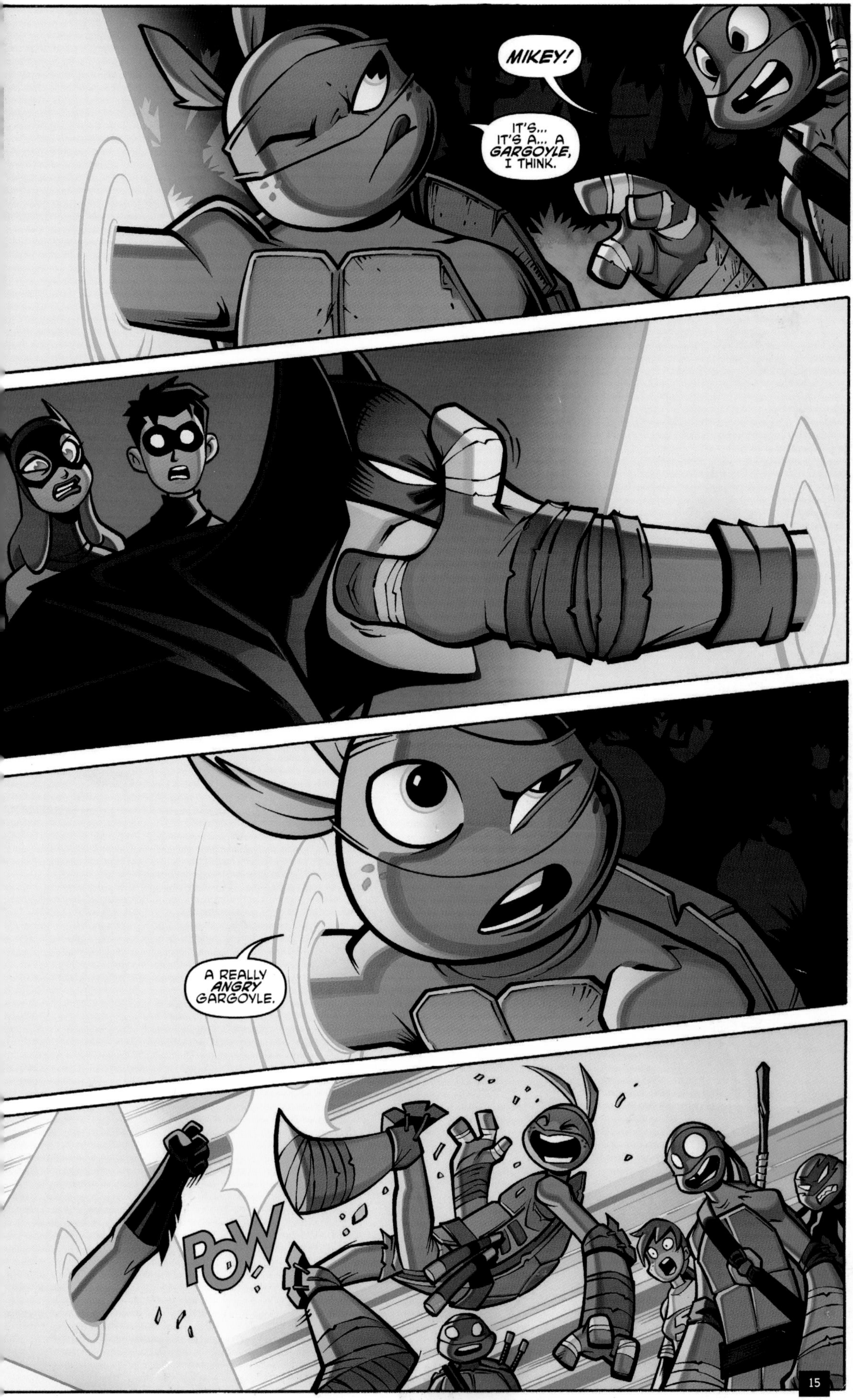
MIKEY!
IT'S... IT'S A... A GARGOYLE, I THINK.
A REALLY ANGRY GARGOYLE.
POW

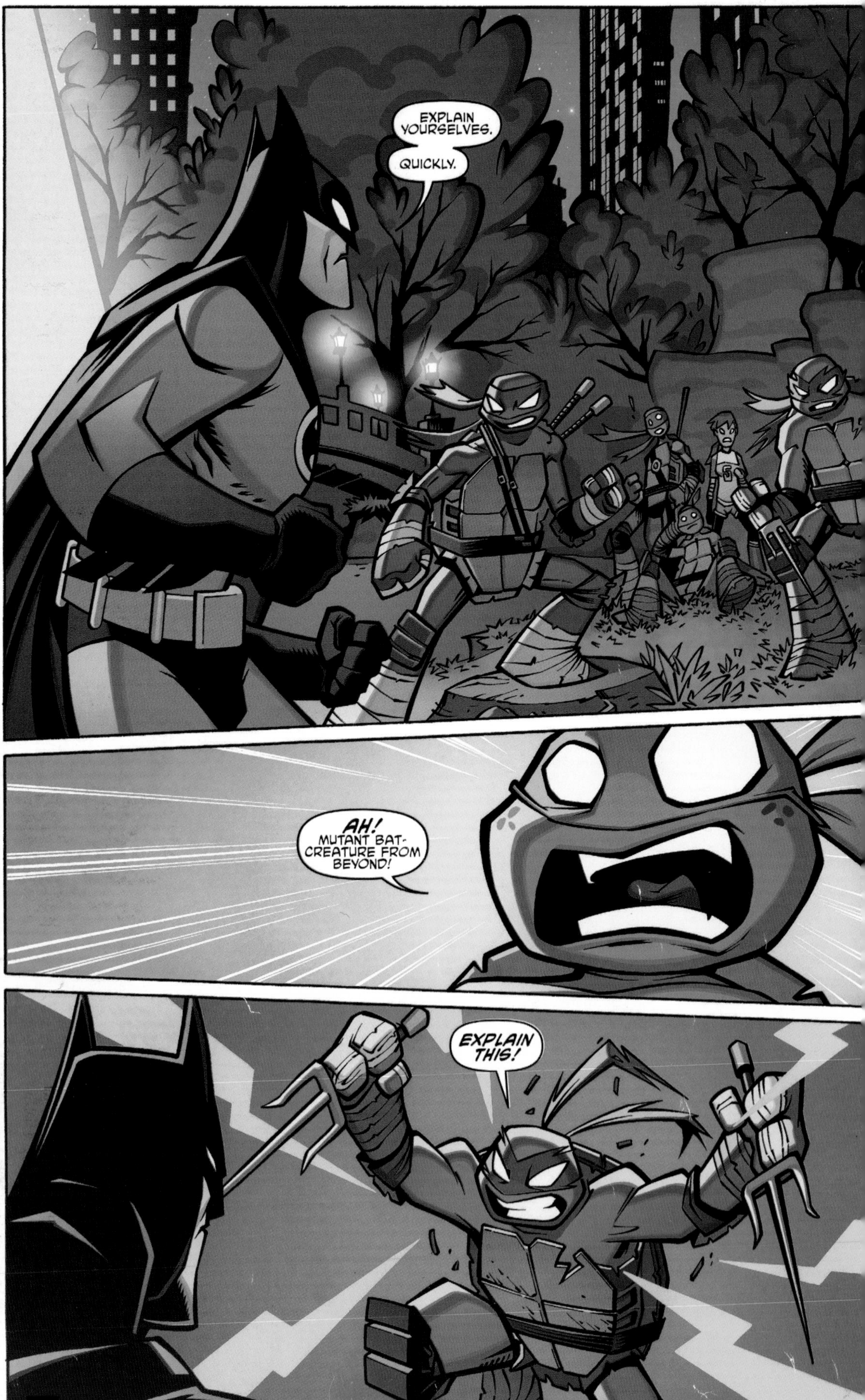
EXPLAIN YOURSELVES.
QUICKLY.
AH! MUTANT BAT-CREATURE FROM BEYOND!
EXPLAIN THIS!

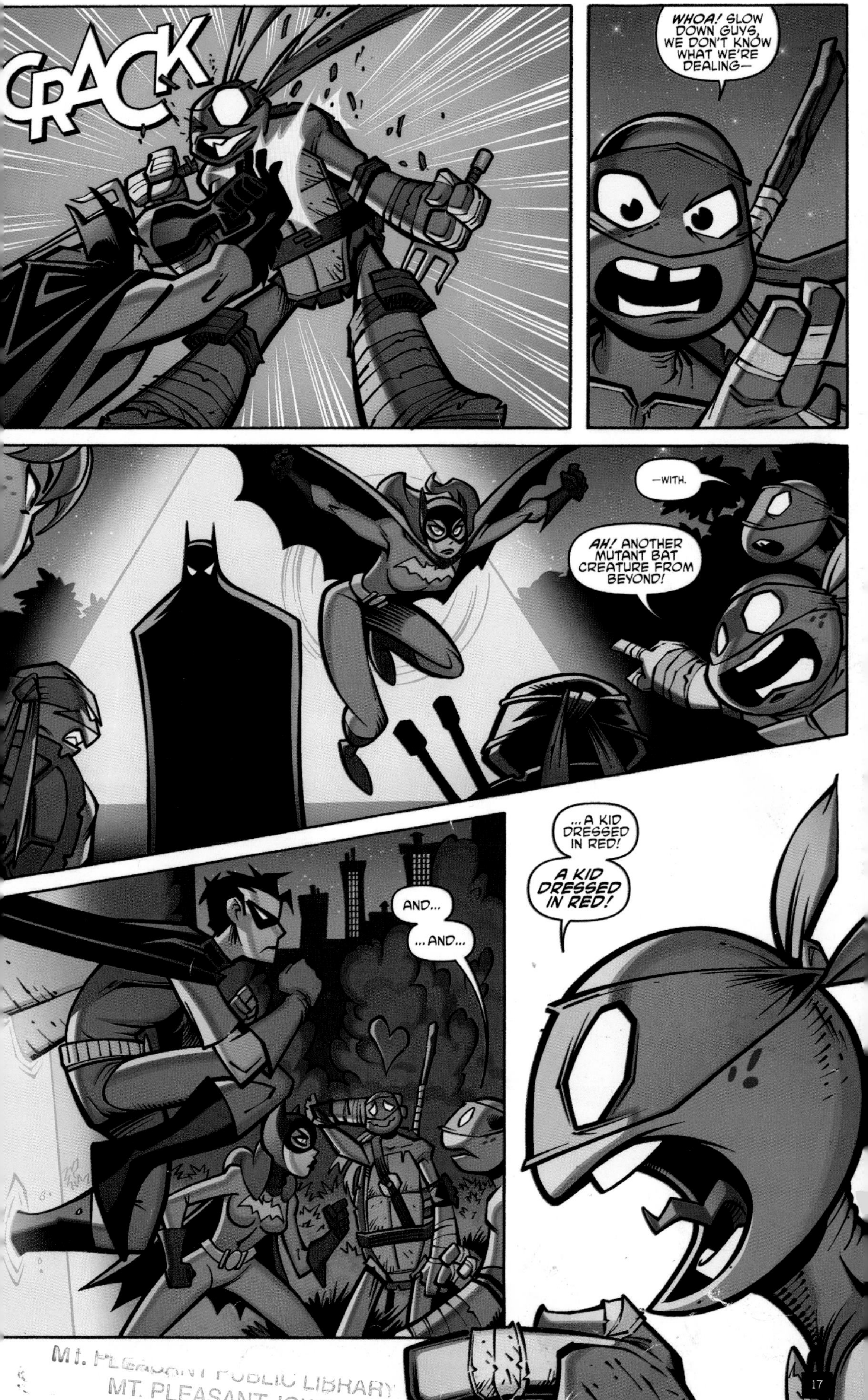
CRACK
WHOA! SLOW DOWN GUYS, WE DON'T KNOW WHAT WE'RE DEALING—
—WITH.
AH! ANOTHER MUTANT BAT CREATURE FROM BEYOND!
AND...
...AND...
...A KID DRESSED IN RED!
A KID DRESSED IN RED!

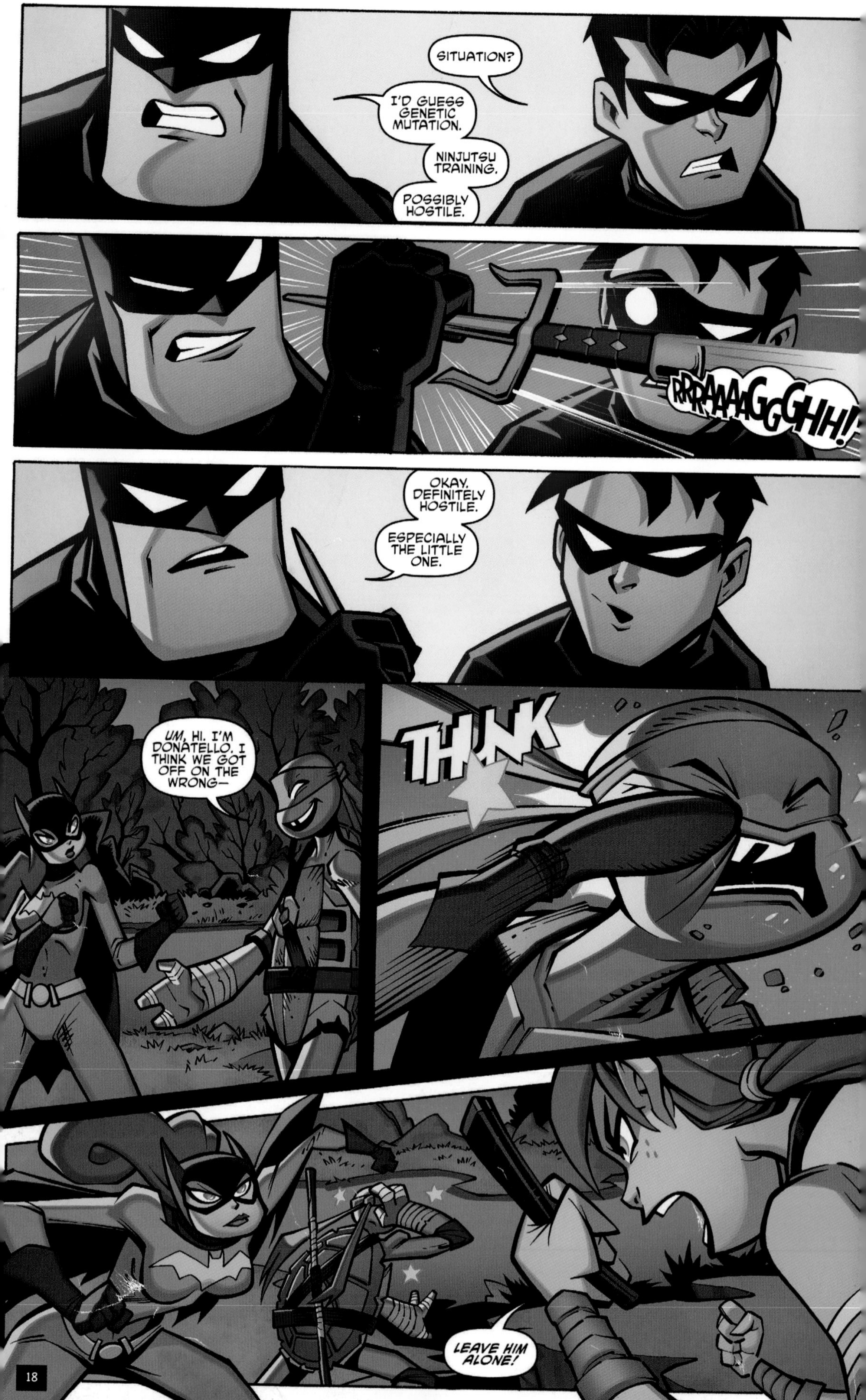

SITUATION?
I'D GUESS GENETIC MUTATION.
NINJUTSU TRAINING.
POSSIBLY HOSTILE.
RRRAAAAGGGHH!
OKAY. DEFINITELY HOSTILE.
ESPECIALLY THE LITTLE ONE.
UM, HI. I'M DONATELLO. I THINK WE GOT OFF ON THE WRONG—
THUNK
LEAVE HIM ALONE!

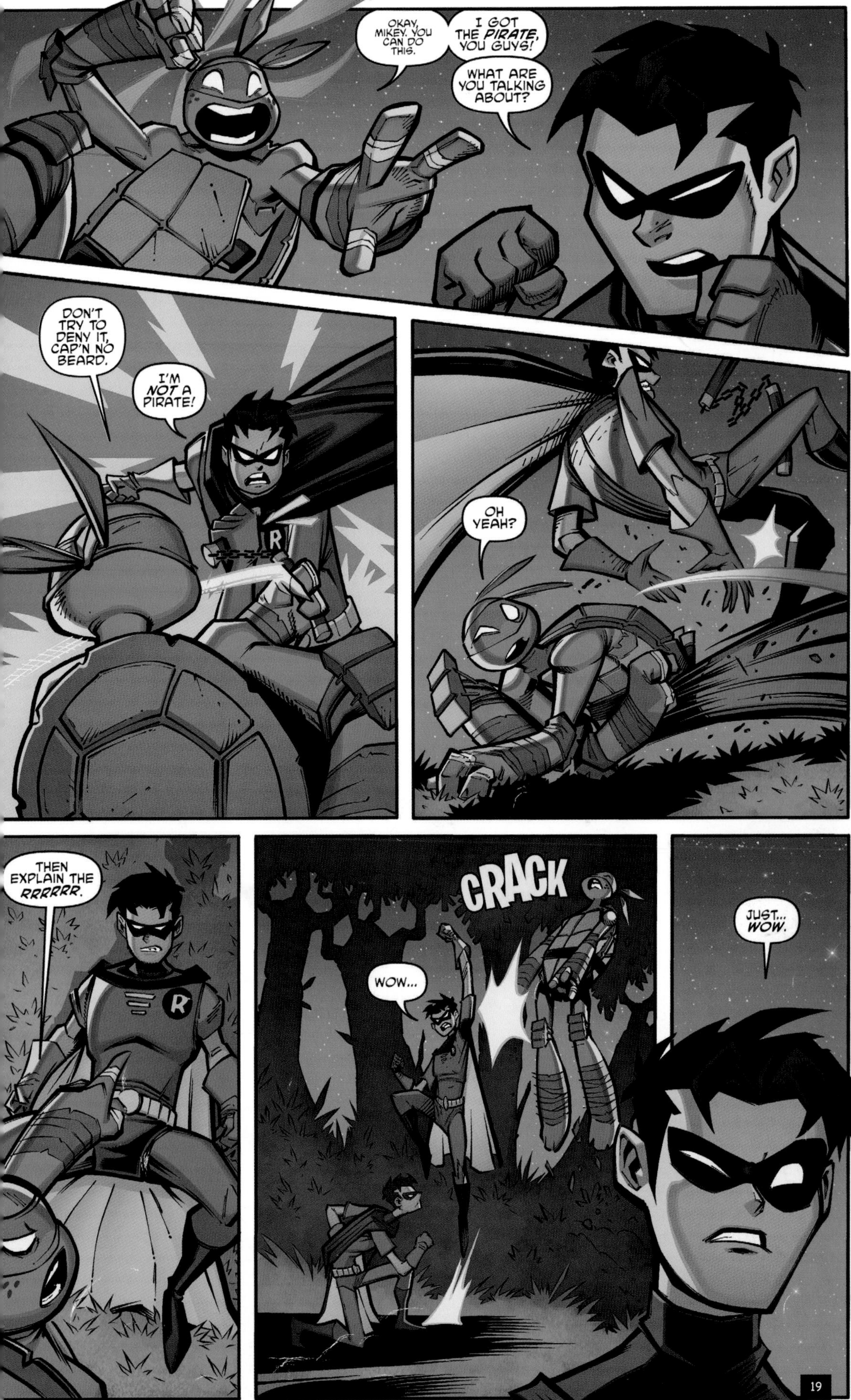

OKAY, MIKEY. YOU CAN DO THIS.
I GOT THE *PIRATE*, YOU GUYS!
WHAT ARE YOU TALKING ABOUT?
DON'T TRY TO DENY IT, CAP'N NO BEARD.
I'M *NOT* A PIRATE!
OH YEAH?
THEN EXPLAIN THE *RRRRRR*.
CRACK
WOW...
JUST... **WOW**.

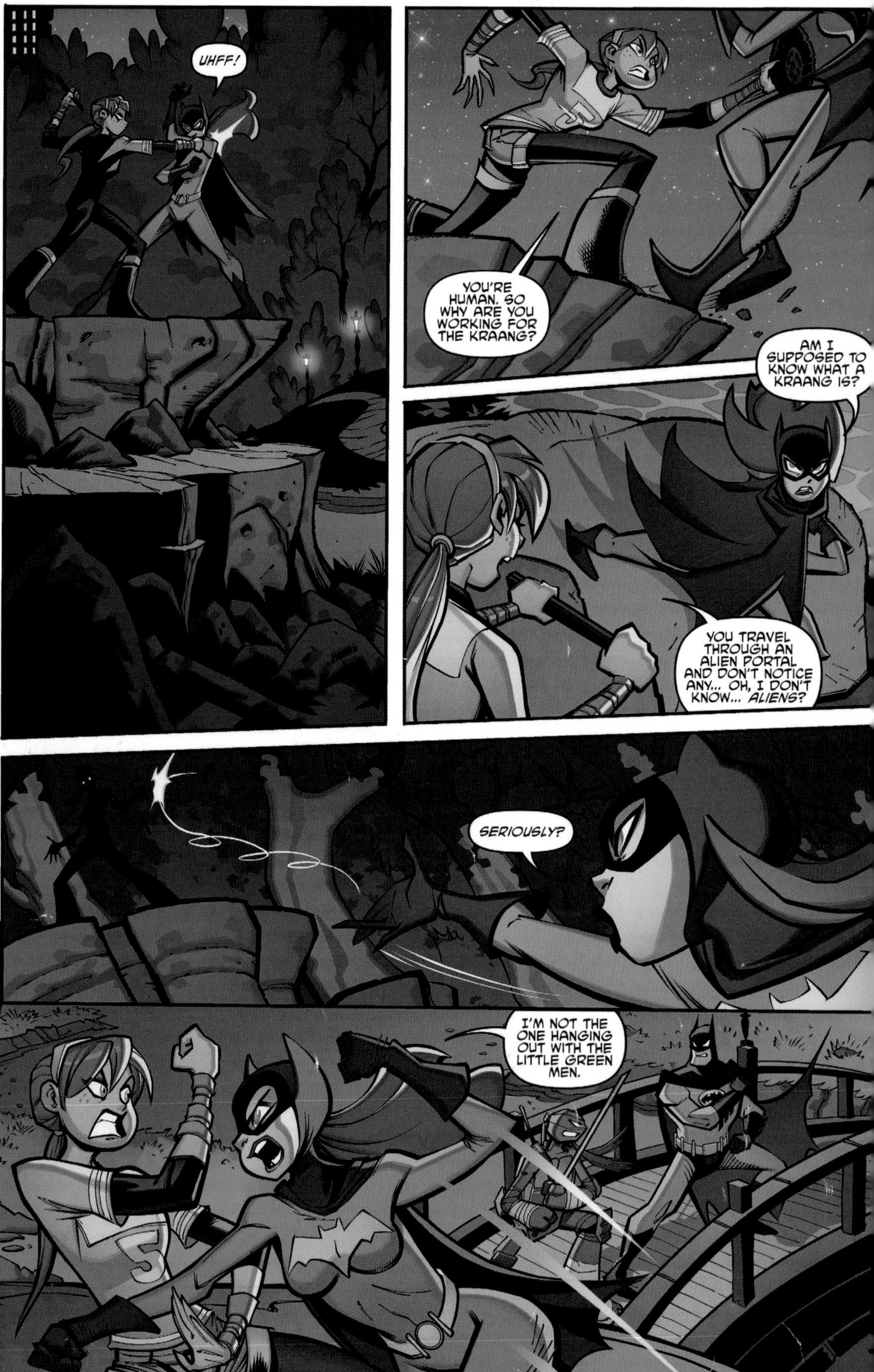
UHFF!
YOU'RE HUMAN. SO WHY ARE YOU WORKING FOR THE KRAANG?
AM I SUPPOSED TO KNOW WHAT A KRAANG IS?
YOU TRAVEL THROUGH AN ALIEN PORTAL AND DON'T NOTICE ANY... OH, I DON'T KNOW... ALIENS?
SERIOUSLY?
I'M NOT THE ONE HANGING OUT WITH THE LITTLE GREEN MEN.

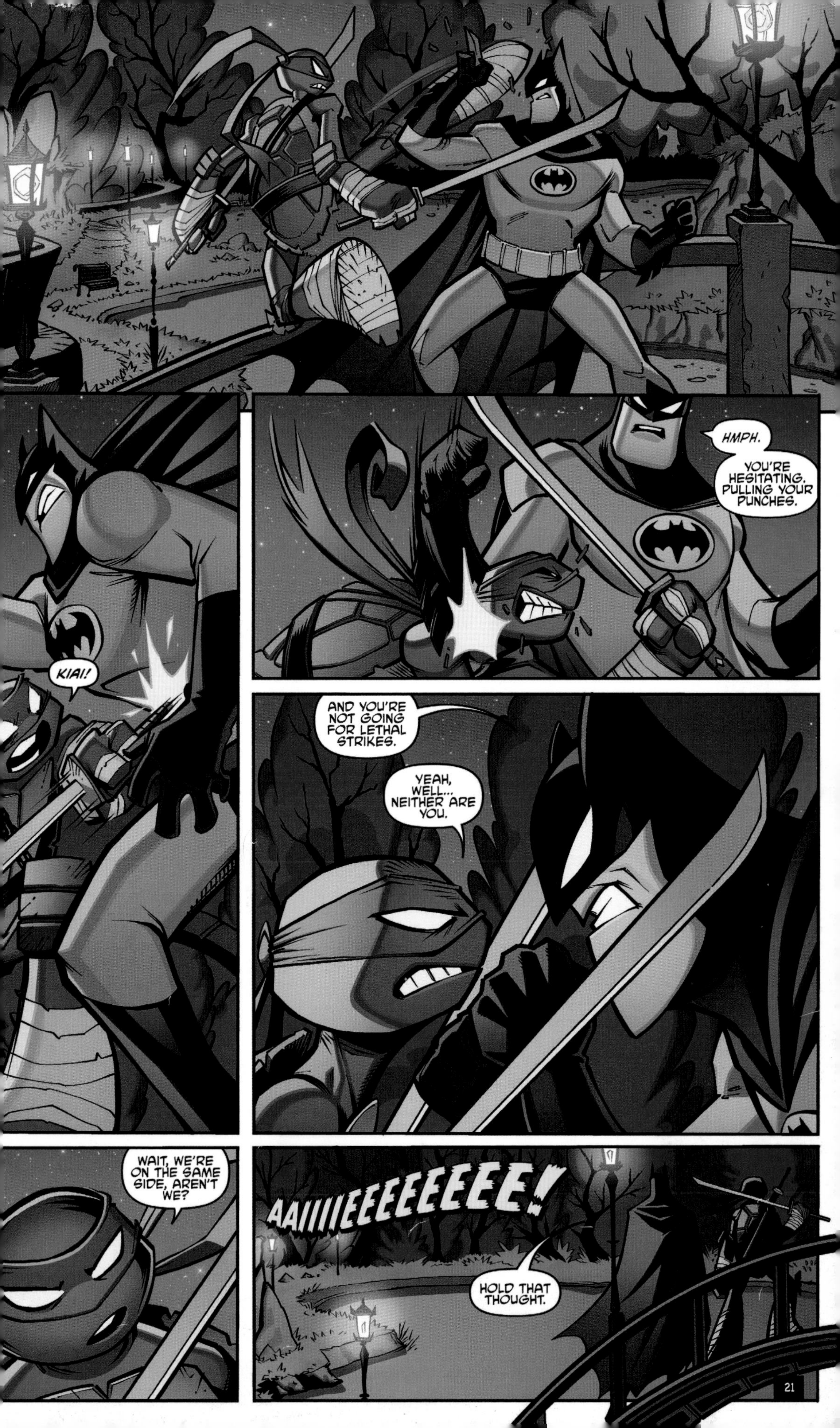
HMPH.
YOU'RE HESITATING. PULLING YOUR PUNCHES.
KIAI!
AND YOU'RE NOT GOING FOR LETHAL STRIKES.
YEAH, WELL... NEITHER ARE YOU.
WAIT, WE'RE ON THE SAME SIDE, AREN'T WE?
AAIIIIIEEEEEEEEE!
HOLD THAT THOUGHT.

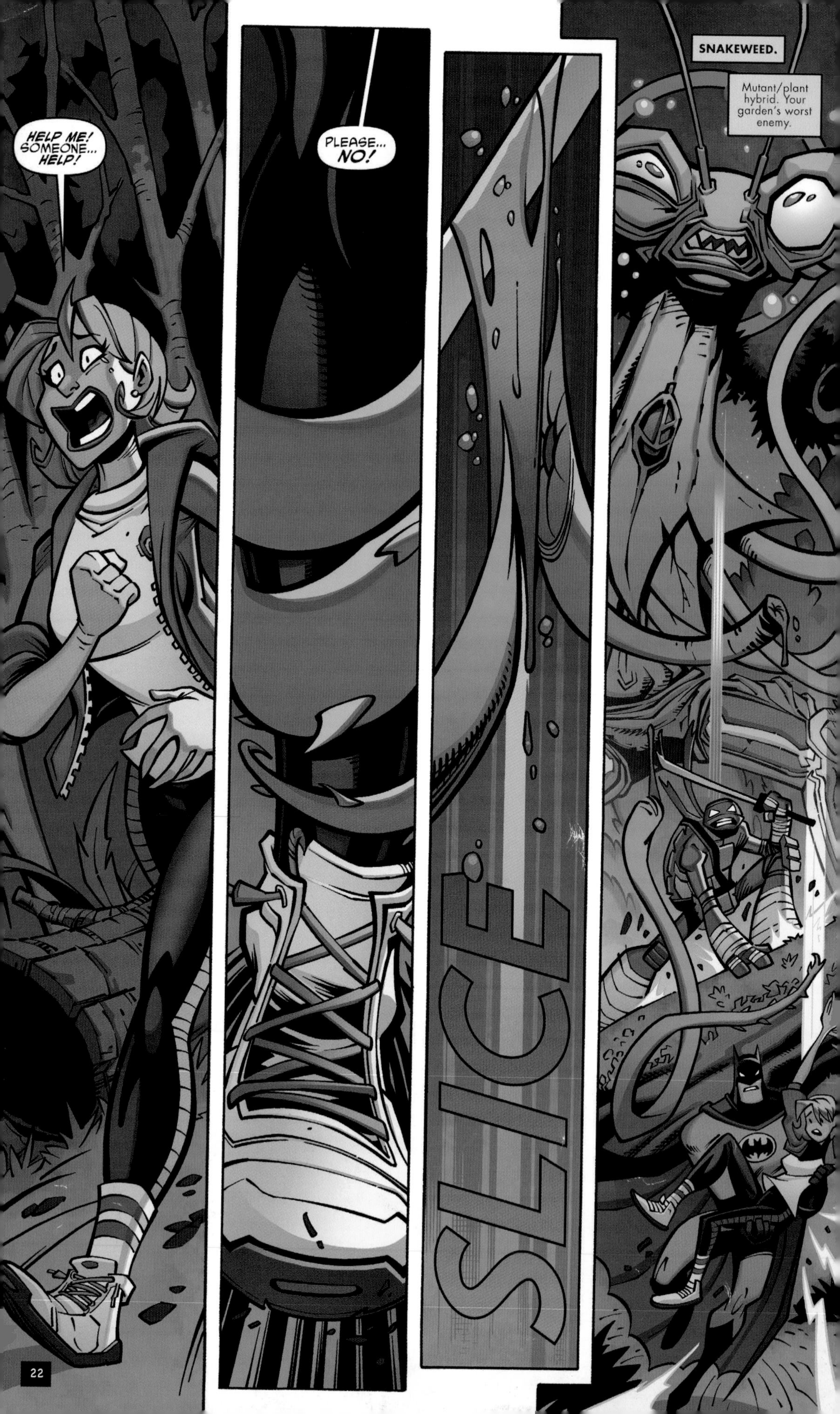
HELP ME! SOMEONE... HELP!
PLEASE... NO!
SLICE
SNAKEWEED.
Mutant/plant hybrid. Your garden's worst enemy.

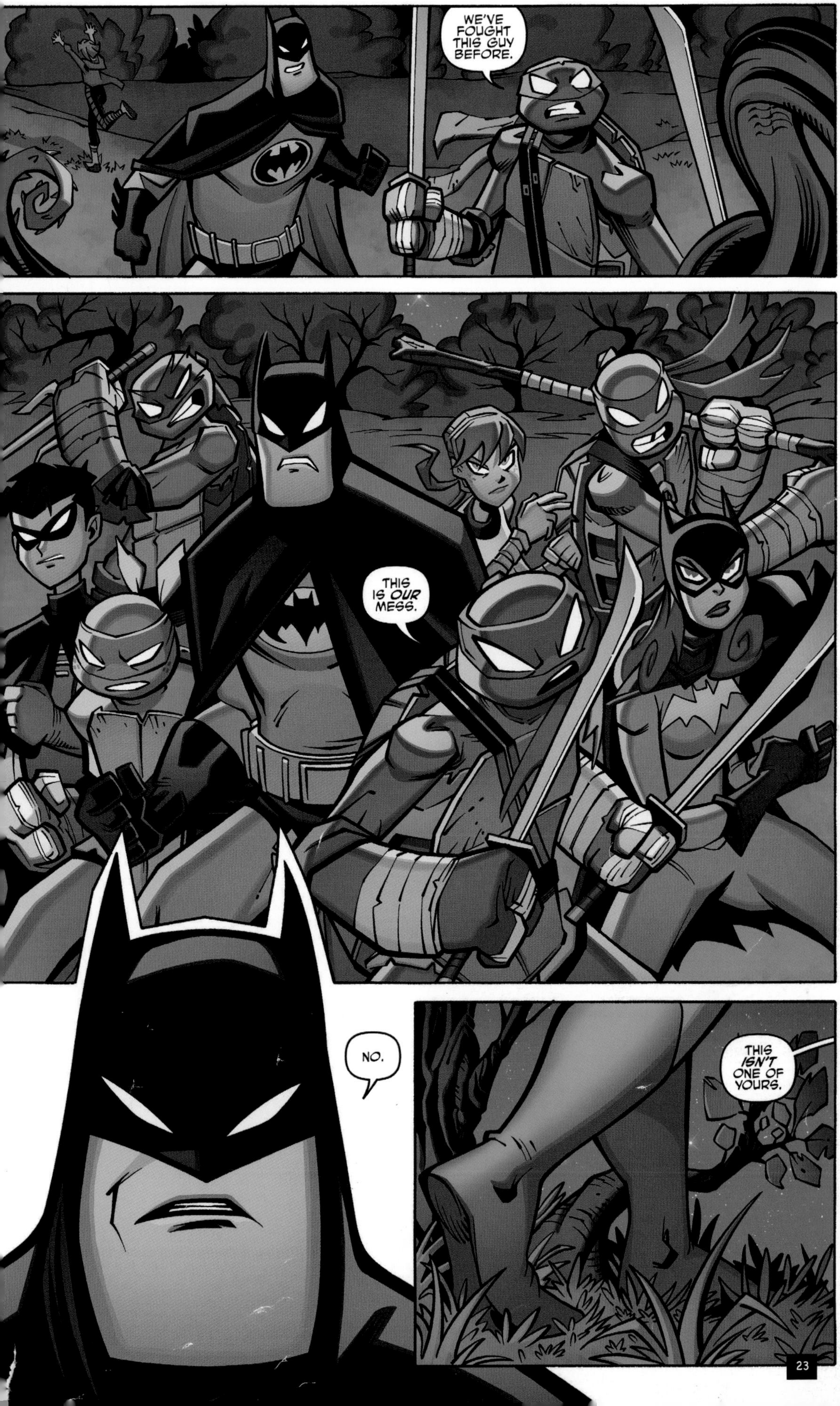

WE'VE FOUGHT THIS GUY BEFORE.
THIS IS *OUR* MESS.
NO.
THIS *ISN'T* ONE OF YOURS.

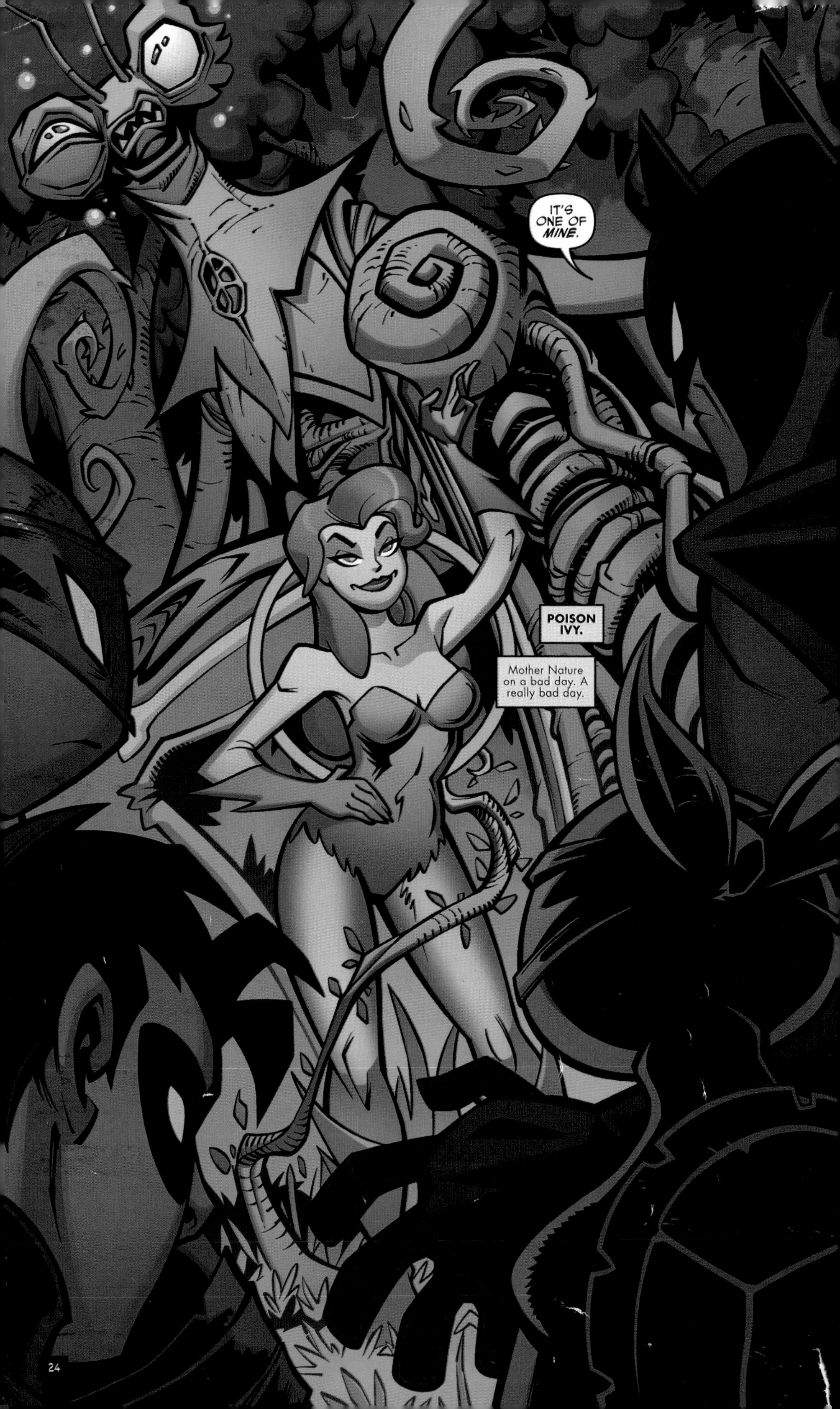

IT'S ONE OF *MINE*.
POISON IVY.
Mother Nature on a bad day. A really bad day.

CREATOR

MATTHEW K. MANNING

THE AUTHOR OF THE AMAZON BEST-SELLING HARDCOVER *BATMAN: A VISUAL HISTORY*, MATTHEW K. MANNING HAS CONTRIBUTED TO MANY COMIC BOOKS, INCLUDING *BEWARE THE BATMAN, SPIDER-MAN UNLIMITED, PIRATES OF THE CARIBBEAN: SIX SEA SHANTIES, JUSTICE LEAGUE ADVENTURES, LOONEY TUNES,* AND *SCOOBY-DOO, WHERE ARE YOU?* WHEN NOT WRITING COMICS, MANNING OFTEN AUTHORS BOOKS ABOUT COMICS, AS WELL AS A SERIES OF YOUNG READER BOOKS STARRING SUPERMAN, BATMAN, AND THE FLASH FOR CAPSTONE. HE CURRENTLY RESIDES IN ASHEVILLE, NORTH CAROLINA, WITH HIS WIFE, DOROTHY, AND THEIR TWO DAUGHTERS, LILLIAN AND GWENDOLYN. VISIT HIM ONLINE AT WWW.MATTHEWKMANNING.COM.

JON SOMMARIVA

JON SOMMARIVA WAS BORN IN SYDNEY, AUSTRALIA. HE HAS BEEN DRAWING COMIC BOOKS SINCE 2002. HIS WORK CAN BE SEEN IN *GEMINI, REXODUS, TMNT ADVENTURES,* AND *STAR WARS ADVENTURES,* AMONG OTHER COMICS. WHEN HE IS NOT DRAWING, HE ENJOYS WATCHING MOVIES AND PLAYING WITH HIS SON, FELIX.

GLOSSARY

adjustment (uh-JUHST-muhnt)—a slight change made to improve something

chock full (CHAHK FUL)—very full or overflowing

creature (KREE-chuhr)—a living being

flair (FLAYR)—style or originality

gargoyle (GAR-goil)—a monsterlike statue built on cathedral churches

hybrid (HYE-brid)—a mix between two different animals or plants

impressive (im-PRESS-iv)—able to gain attention or admiration

interdimensional (in-tur-duh-MIN-shuhn-ul)—between two different
realities or parallel universes

klutz (KLUHTS)—a clumsy person

method (METH-uhd)—a way of doing things

mutant (MYOOT-uhnt)—a living thing that has developed different
characteristics than its parents had

ninjutsu (nihn-JIHT-soo)—the skills and fighting technique involved with being
a ninja

panache (PUH-nash)—a display of confidence in style or manner

patience (PAY-shuhnss)—being able to put up with problems that usually
cause anger

spectacular (spek-TAK-yuh-lur)—remarkable or dramatic

upholstery (uhp-HOL-stur-ee)—the stuffing, cushions, and covering on
a chair

VISUAL QUESTIONS AND WRITING PROMPTS

1. WHY DID THE JOKER SPEND SO MUCH TIME REARRANGING THE GUARDS? HINT: TAKE ANOTHER LOOK AT PAGE 8.

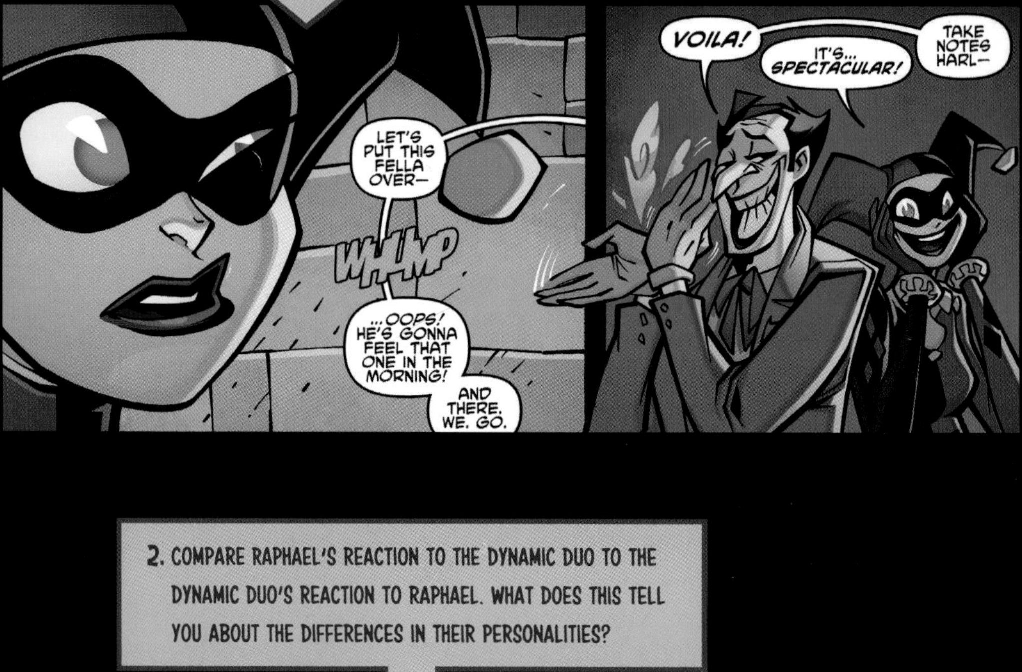
LET'S PUT THIS FELLA OVER—
WHUMP
...OOPS! HE'S GONNA FEEL THAT ONE IN THE MORNING!
AND THERE. WE. GO.
VOILA!
IT'S... SPECTACULAR!
TAKE NOTES HARL—

2. COMPARE RAPHAEL'S REACTION TO THE DYNAMIC DUO TO THE DYNAMIC DUO'S REACTION TO RAPHAEL. WHAT DOES THIS TELL YOU ABOUT THE DIFFERENCES IN THEIR PERSONALITIES?

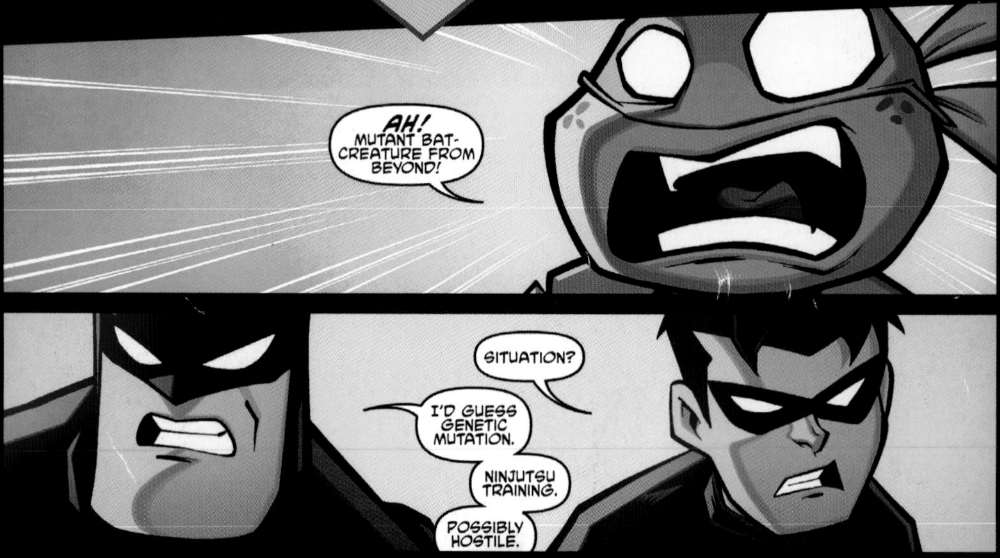
AH! MUTANT BAT-CREATURE FROM BEYOND!
SITUATION?
I'D GUESS GENETIC MUTATION.
NINJUTSU TRAINING.
POSSIBLY HOSTILE.

3. PRETEND THAT RAPHAEL DIDN'T ATTACK BATMAN, AND REWRITE THIS SCENE. THEN DRAW YOUR OWN PANELS TO GO WITH IT.

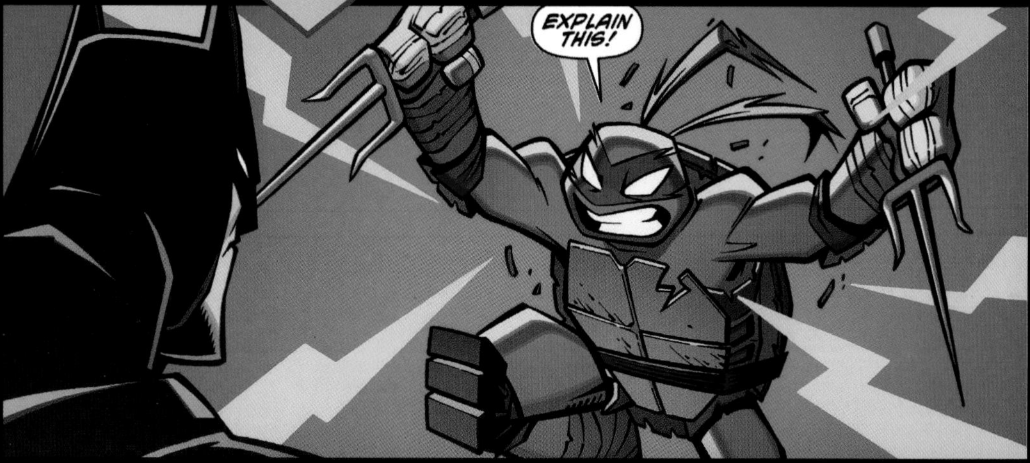
EXPLAIN THIS!

4. DESCRIBE DONATELLO'S FACIAL EXPRESSION IN THE PANEL BELOW. WHAT DOES THIS TELL YOU ABOUT HOW HE'LL BEHAVE FOR THE REST OF THE BOOK?

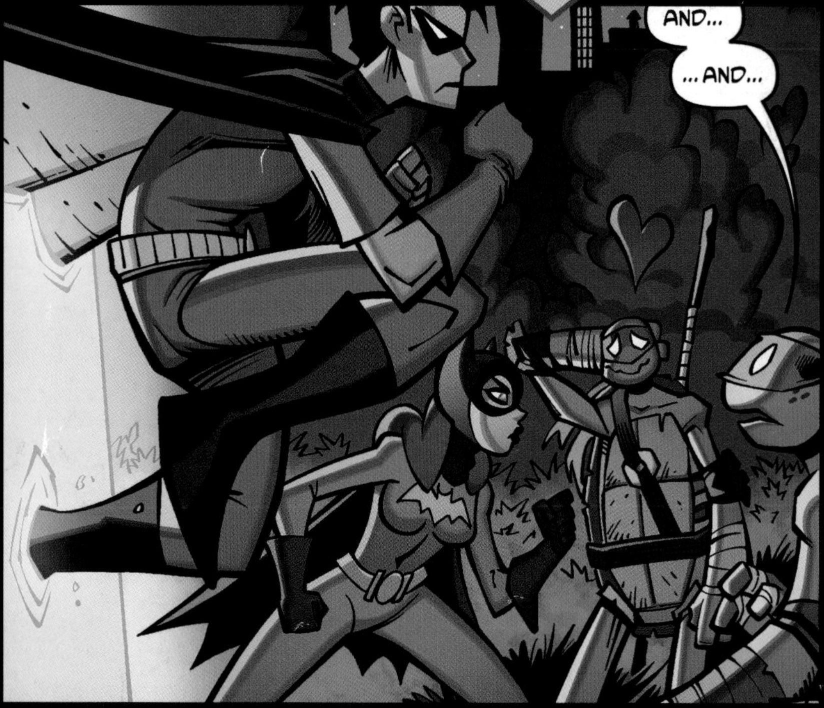
AND...
...AND...

BATMAN TEENAGE MUTANT NINJA TURTLES ADVENTURES

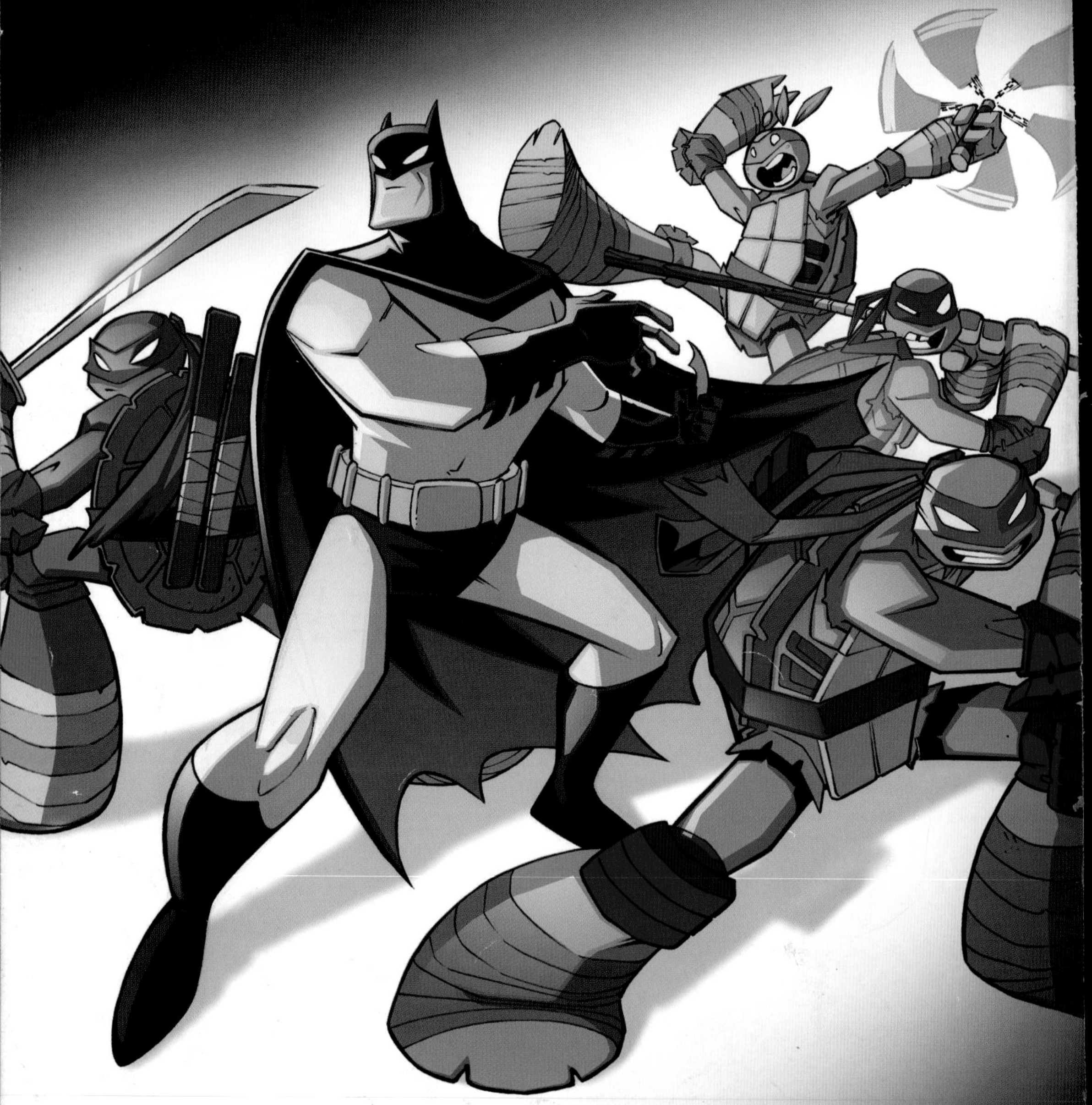

READ THEM ALL!

IDW
BATMAN
TEENAGE MUTANT NINJA TURTLES
ADVENTURES
THE FACE OF TWO WORLDS

IDW
BATMAN
TEENAGE MUTANT NINJA TURTLES
ADVENTURES
THE CLOWN AND THE CLAN

IDW
BATMAN
TEENAGE MUTANT NINJA TURTLES
ADVENTURES
GREENER ON THE OTHER SIDE

IDW
BATMAN
TEENAGE MUTANT NINJA TURTLES
ADVENTURES
TO LAUGH SO NOT TO CRY

IDW
BATMAN
TEENAGE MUTANT NINJA TURTLES
ADVENTURES
THROUGH THE LOOKING GLASS

IDW
BATMAN
TEENAGE MUTANT NINJA TURTLES
ADVENTURES
THE TERROR OF THE KRAANG

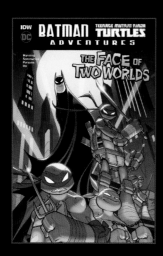

BATMAN TEENAGE MUTANT NINJA TURTLES

ADVENTURES